INCONVENIENT LOVE

INCONVENIENT LOVE

JOYCE VALDOIS SMITH

TALLGRASS
MEDIA

Inconvenient Love
Copyright © 2021 by Joyce Valdois Smith

Published by Tallgrass Media
books@tallgrass.media
www.tallgrass.media

Cover and interior book design by Kelly Smith.
Cover montage photograph by Erik Smith.

Paperback ISBN: 978-1-956589-01-6

To Bob, my husband and best friend of fifty-one years. During the COVID-19 lockdown, I came to appreciate you even more than ever. We found that we not only loved each other, but we liked being together. Thank you for your support of my writing and for traveling with me to do research for my books. I couldn't ask for anyone better.

To my children and their spouses: Kelly & Joice, Janna & Michael, Annette & Andrew, and Holly & Erik. You are all special to me. I find great joy in being a Mom and thank you all for your love and encouragement.

To my awesome grandchildren: Gabby and her husband, Spencer, Isaiah, Rylee, Aidan, Ridge, Sophie, April, Michaela, Sonja, Carenza, Blakeney, Dani, and Landry. I am so proud of your lives, your accomplishments, and your Christian testimonies! I thank the Lord for you and pray for you every day.

To Pastor Chadd and Morgen Harkrider. With God's guidance, you shepherded our church through the difficult period of shutdowns, Zoom meetings, and live-streaming services. Thank you for your faithfulness.

CHAPTER 1

"I can do this. I can do this." Tessa Gillespie muttered the words as she stared out the train window. All she could see from horizon to horizon was a rolling prairie with tall grass waving in the wind. It'd rained most of the day. The gray sky matched her mood.

A mantle of homesickness settled around her shoulders, and a lump of pain took up residence in her throat. She'd just said goodbye to her best friend, Elise Dumond, at the Harvey House in Emporia, Kansas. They'd met a month earlier at their Harvey Girl interviews and even in such a short time had grown close. They lived, worked, and played together as they trained to be Harvey Girls. How would she move on to another house without Elise's support?

Tessa leaned her head against the back of the seat and let her mind wander back to her family in Arkansas. Was it only a month ago that she'd left to travel to Kansas City? It seemed much longer than that. Her chest contracted at the thought of her parents, five younger sisters, and little brother as they stood on the train platform and waved goodbye. When would she see them again?

"Next stop, Hutchinson, Kansas," the conductor announced as he walked through the train car. He stopped at each seat. "Meals will be served in the Harvey House dining room and lunchroom. Do you plan to dine during this stop?"

Tessa nodded. "In the lunchroom. I'll stay in Hutchinson. I'm the new Harvey Girl."

"I'm glad to meet you." He marked on his paper.

She looked across the aisle to her friends, Caroline and Abigail. "They're Harvey Girls, too. We finished training in Topeka and are traveling to our new assignments."

He pivoted to them. "Where will you girls work?"

Caroline spoke up. "I'm going to Las Vegas, New Mexico, and she'll be in La Junta, Colorado. We'll eat in the lunchroom and spend the night. Tomorrow we head to our destinations."

The conductor nodded then moved up the aisle.

"I wish one of you could stay here, too." Tessa pursed her lips. "I won't know anyone."

Caroline smiled at her. "It'd be nice if we could stay together, but you'll be alright. It won't take long to get acquainted with the new Harvey Girls."

Tessa sighed. "I know, but I'm going to miss you and Abigail."

"We'll all be in the same situation."

Tessa leaned over and looked out the window as the train whistle sounded, an indication they were getting close. Houses appeared along the tracks, huddled closer together as they entered the outskirts of town. They passed clapboard buildings that looked like warehouses. A wooden sign at the side of the tracks proclaimed, "Hutchinson, Kansas."

The train slowed and pulled to a stop beside the red brick depot. A loud hiss sounded as the engine let off steam. The conductor announced, from the back of the car, "The depot is on your left and the Santa Fe Hotel and Harvey House are to the right and across Main Street."

Tessa grabbed her carpetbag and stepped from the train. Caroline and Abigail followed. A light mist fell. They all hesitated as a loud gong sounded from a majestic, three-story brick Queen-Anne-style building north of the track. There were gables with peaked roofs and a white wrap-around porch. It bordered the west side of Main Street.

"Wow!" Tessa stared. "Is that the Harvey House? It's amazing."

"It is charming." Abigail started toward the building. "Come on, we're getting wet, and I'm hungry."

They followed the other passengers as they hurried to the Harvey House. A young boy was standing on the porch hitting a gong with a padded stick and yelling at the top of his voice. "Right this way, folks. Harvey House dining room. Come on in."

The three of them walked into the spacious lobby.

Inside, a man wearing a black suit stood and greeted the people from the train. As the girls approached, he paused. "May I help you?"

Tessa stepped forward. "Yes, we're Harvey Girls. I'm Tessa Gillespie. I'm assigned here."

"Very well. We've expected you. I'm Mr. McKinsey, the Harvey House manager." He looked at Caroline and Abigail. "I understand you'll spend the night then go on tomorrow." He gestured toward the dining room. "Cora Dickenson is our head waitress. She'll take care of you."

Tessa, Caroline, and Abigail walked across the lobby where Cora, dressed in the typical black and white uniform, greeted other patrons. When there was a break, she turned toward them. "Hello, are you my new Harvey Girls?"

Caroline gestured at Tessa with her thumb. "She is. Abigail and I are just here for the night."

Cora nodded. "So I understand. Go eat in the lunchroom. I'll talk with you more after we're through serving."

Tessa stepped through the door. The lunchroom was more spacious than it appeared from the outside. A large semi-circular counter took up most of the area. Harvey Girls busily set up their stations and took drink orders.

Caroline, Abigail, and Tessa chose seats along one side of the counter. Tessa sat beside a young girl who struck her as seven or eight years old. The child reminded Tessa of her little sister, Lucile. The girl had barely touched the food on her plate. She swiveled her seat back and forth pushing against the counter with her feet. A man, presumably her father, who sat three seats away, turned to her. "Esther Marie, quit dawdling and eat. We need to leave shortly so Anthony and I can feed the livestock before dark."

At that point, a Harvey Girl approached the counter where Tessa and her friends were seated. "What would you like to drink?"

"I'll have iced tea." Tessa picked up the menu and perused the entrees. The baked ham and sweet potato casserole looked good.

She didn't want to stare, but it was hard to ignore the drama unfolding beside her. Esther picked up her fork, stabbed a small bite of potato, and stuffed it in her mouth. Then she laid her fork back down and began to swivel her chair again.

Two other small children sat between Esther and the man. The first was a girl, maybe four, and a boy who looked about two or three. He was wiggling on his seat. He stood and launched himself into his father's lap.

"Charlie, you have to sit on your stool. I need to finish

eating." The man set Charlie firmly down on the seat. Charlie puckered up and let out an ear-piercing wail.

Cora appeared behind them. "Come on, Charlie. Why don't you come and help me." She picked him up and set him on her hip then turned to the man. "It's been a long day, Cliff. He's tired. You finish eating. I'll keep him until you're through."

The four-year-old slid off the stool. "Can I come, too, Aunt Cora?"

"Sure, come on, Anna. Give your daddy a little peace."

"I wanna go." Esther started to scoot off.

"No, you stay here. You need to eat. You'll be hungry before bedtime." Her father pushed her back onto the stool.

Esther frowned as Cora walked away with the two littlest ones.

Tessa ordered her meal, then peered out of the corner of her eye at the man Cora had called Cliff. He was maybe in his late twenties...early thirties, long legs, muscular arms, and tanned skin, obviously from outside work. His dark brown hair reached his collar and showed a sweat ring where his cowboy hat had been. Button-up shirt, blue jeans, and boots gave testimony that he was a cattleman. His most remarkable features were his deep brown eyes. Although he looked tired, he'd been patient with the little ones. At this moment, he was devouring the large plate of food in front of him. When he finished, he waved to the Harvey Girl. "Hannah, can you give me something to wrap Esther's sandwich in. I know she'll be hungry before bedtime, and I don't want to fix something later."

"Sure." Hannah returned with a large piece of heavy paper and a length of a string. She placed Esther's food on the paper and wrapped it then tied the string around it.

"Thank you." He turned to the young teenage boy on his

other side. "You finished, Anthony? We better get home. The milk cows will be bawlin' their heads off."

Anthony slipped off the stool. "Yeah, I'm ready."

Cliff lifted Esther down. "Here carry your food." He walked to the lunchroom door and the others followed.

Hannah placed Tessa's plate in front of her. "I'm sorry for the delay. Cliff's a widower. His wife died when Charlie was born. We try to help him as much as possible when he comes in. His wife was Cora's sister."

"Ohhh… I'm sorry to hear that. The children are about the same age as my sisters and brother." Tessa placed her napkin in her lap. "They seem well-behaved."

"They're obedient, for the most part. Of course, they're just kids." She surveyed Caroline and Abigail. "Are you the new Harvey Girls?"

"Yes." Tessa held up her hand. "My name's Tessa. I'll be here. Abigail's going to Colorado and Caroline's headed to New Mexico."

"I'm excited to meet you all." Hannah faced Tessa. "My former roommate transferred to Arizona so you and I will be roommates. We can talk after I get through. Right now, I better get busy." She picked up the used dishes the young family had left and cleaned the counter for the next customers.

After they ate, Tessa, Caroline, and Abigail strolled into the lobby. Cora sat at a table and collected money from the departing patrons. "I'll be with you girls and show you to your rooms as soon as I get through."

Tessa gazed around the spacious lobby. Large walnut beams spanned the ceiling and pillars were situated along the length of the room. Polished hardwood floors were accented by colorful rugs and groupings of chairs. Sofas were arranged artfully around the room. An ornate reception desk sat at the back of the lobby near a massive staircase. The banisters were fashioned from the same dark walnut as the pillars, all polished to a warm glow.

The girls chose chairs near the reception desk. After the local customers left the dining room, Cora strolled over to visit with them. "Follow me and I'll take you to your rooms. The Harvey Girl residence is on the third floor and hotel rooms are on the second." She led them up the stairway past the first landing. A parlor was at the top of the third-floor stairs. It was an open room with windows along the back. A fire burned in the large fireplace and gas lights in sconces were lit around the walls. Chairs, similar to those in the main lobby, were placed in groupings throughout the room. A large grand piano sat in the corner. Brightly painted pictures gave color and character to the room.

Cora paused. "We don't normally have a fire lit in the fireplace in the summer, but this rain has put a chill in the air." She turned to the right. "Our rooms are on this end. The men have rooms on the west wing. The parlor's the dividing line." She grinned. "As you know, the gentlemen's area is strictly off-limits."

They walked through the door into the dormitory corridor. "Tessa, you will be in the second room on the right. Hannah Johnson's your roommate. The busboy brings the baggage from the depot, so your trunk will have arrived by now. "

As they entered the room, rain lashed against the south windows. The room was furnished almost identical to the rooms in the Topeka Harvey House. Cora pointed to the bed on the right. "This will be your side. See, your trunk's at the end of your bed."

She turned toward Caroline and Abigail. "You'll stay in the room at the end of the hall. We've supplied sheets and blankets from the hotel for you to use tonight." She looked out the window. "I hope this rain lets up. Traveling tomorrow will be unpleasant if it doesn't. It's been so dry. We needed the rain, but not floods." She motioned toward the door. "Here, I'll show you two to your room."

Tessa set about unpacking her trunk. She made her bed and hung her clothes in the wardrobe. She was nearly finished when Hannah walked in.

CLIFF CLAPPED his hat on his head and stepped onto the porch of the Harvey House with his brood. He shook his head. The rain was pouring off the eaves in sheets. "Anthony, you stay here with the girls. I'll take Charlie and bring the carriage up as close to the door as possible. You'll have to make a run for it."

"Okay, Pa."

Cliff hiked Charlie up onto his hip then took off his hat and placed it on Charlie's head. "Hang on, buddy." He ducked his head and sprinted down the boardwalk toward the parking area. The lot was already a loblolly of mud and water. He'd stay in town if it weren't for cows that needed to be milked. Not an option. He picked his way around the puddles to his family carriage. Thankfully, he'd attached the side curtains before they left that morning.

He'd left the younguns with their Grandma Dickenson while he and Anthony had gone to the livestock auction earlier that day. He'd bought ten yearling steers and another milk cow with her calf. He was slowly building his herd. If this rain let up, he'd put the sides on the wagon and come get them tomorrow.

He sat Charlie on the carriage seat, unhitched his mare, Babe, and climbed up beside his son. Babe stomped her hooves in the mud. "You don't like this any better than I do, do you, Babe?" He pulled on the reins and backed away from the hitching post then drove out onto the road in front of the Santa Fe Hotel.

Anthony picked up Anna and held onto Esther's hand as they ran toward the carriage. "Think we can make it home, Pa?"

"We have to. The cows have to be milked. I'll drive across the pastures. It'll be easier going on the grass than the muddy road."

An hour later--double the usual time--they drove up the drive of their homestead. Cliff had detoured around water that was running across the road and traversed the prairie and pastures to keep from getting stuck. Relief flowed through him at the sight of their wood-frame house.

Soaked to his skin, he jumped down and scooted the little ones inside. "Don't forget your food, Esther." He lit the lantern in the kitchen and stoked up the fire in the wood cookstove. The cold rain made the house cool and damp. "Esther, help Anna and Charlie get out of their wet clothes and into pajamas. You get ready for bed, too. Anthony and I will be in as soon as we get the livestock fed and the cows milked."

Esther wrinkled her nose. "Do I have to? Why do I have ta do all the work?"

"You know better than that. You don't do all the work. Anna and Charlie can't do things themselves. They need help and I have to be out in the barn."

"I can do it my own self!" Anna lifted her chin. "Esther doesn't have to help me get my jammies on."

"I do it." Charlie piped up.

Cliff grinned. "Now, Charlie, I think you need some help. You can take your clothes off like a champion, but putting them on is another story." He grabbed the second lantern, lit it, and carried it into the children's bedroom. He and Anthony each had a separate room. "We'll be back soon. Stay out of trouble."

He grabbed the milk bucket from the back porch and let himself out the kitchen door. The rain had let up some. Anthony had driven the carriage to the shed and was leading Babe across the yard to the barn.

Anthony and Esther had had to take on more responsibility than they should have at such an early age. Anthony had just turned thirteen, but he worked as hard as any farmhand. Cliff sighed as he strode across the yard. It certainly wasn't a piece of cake to raise four young children on his own. He glanced at the overcast sky. *Lord, if you could see fit, I'd sure like to have a help-mate. I miss Ella fiercely, but I know she's in Heaven with you. I couldn't ask her to come back. It's been two and a half years. I'm pretty sure she'd want me to move on.*

He frowned slightly as the vision of the attractive, brown-eyed young woman with blonde hair, who had sat next to them at the lunch counter, flashed through his mind. She had seemed so interested in his family. Probably a train passenger or a hotel guest, so the chance of seeing her again was slim to none.

When he reached the barn, Anthony had driven the cows into their stanchions. "They were waiting to get in. I'm glad I didn't have to go look for them."

"I am too. No fun in this rain."

Cliff lifted the one-legged stool from the peg on the wall, placed it beside the first cow's udders, and balanced on it. He touched her hindquarters with his hand. "So, Bossy, steady now. We'll get you some relief just as quickly as we can." He squirted milk into the bucket in two steady streams while Anthony put grain in the feed troughs. A mama cat and her three kittens rubbed his legs impatiently waiting for some of the fresh, warm milk.

Charlie and Anna were asleep when he and Anthony returned to the house with a brimming bucket of milk. Esther sat at the table and nibbled her Harvey House sandwich while reading a book. The brown paper and string lay on the table beside her.

Cliff set the milk on the cabinet. He stretched a clean piece of cheesecloth over a crockery jug. "Here, Esther. Can you come and hold this while I strain the milk through it? I need to get it into the icebox."

She nodded and went to help. After the milk was run through, he touched her shoulder. "Thank you for your help, Sweetie. I appreciate you putting the little ones to bed."

She settled again to finish her meal. "You're welcome, Papa."

CHAPTER 2

The next morning Tessa stood on the porch and waved goodbye to her friends as they boarded the train. Cora was beside her. "I know it's hard to see your friends leave, but I bet you'll be fine. I remember that feeling. We have a great bunch of girls and friendly staff here. You've already met quite a few of them. And this is a nice town."

Tessa nodded and watched until the train was out of sight. A misty rain still fell so it hid her tears as she turned to follow Cora inside. "I like this House. I know I'll be alright. I enjoyed my visit with Hannah last night. We'll get along famously."

"Good. I thought you would." Cora started toward the lunchroom. "We better get back to work. The other girls can show you your section of the lunch counter. You'll find we're very busy at breakfast and lunch. We have a good number of local business people, railroad employees, and ranchers who eat here besides the train crowds. Some of them like to sit and visit as they drink their coffee. She paused and turned toward Tessa with a smile. "When you feel ready you can serve the meal to Mr. McKinsey and me. Then we'll schedule you in the dining room."

As Tessa entered the lunchroom, Carrie, one of the girls, pointed toward the coffee pots. "Can you fill drinks for us? That would help."

"Sure." Tessa hurried behind the counter and picked up the silver coffee carafe and water pitcher. She kept busy filling cups and glasses until the last customer had left.

Hannah approached her. "Have you met all these girls?" She swung her arm to indicate the lunchroom Harvey Girls.

Tessa shook her head. "I've met a couple, Carrie and Maxine, and of course, you, but not the others."

"These two are Sarah and Lucy." Hannah indicated the other two girls. "Here's your section of the lunch counter. If you have questions about where the supplies are stored, don't hesitate to ask. We'll be glad to help. It won't take long to have it all down pat."

"Thank you. I appreciate your help."

Sarah grabbed a mop from the dish room. "I wish this rain would stop. We need to get the muddy footprints cleaned up. You never know when Fred Harvey might show up and he doesn't tolerate any untidiness."

Cora walked in. "When it rains here, it pours! I wish we could spread it out over the next few months. I just got word that some of the track has washed out on the other side of Dodge City. Your friends might have a delay, Tessa."

"Oh, dear. I hope they're able to get to their new houses."

"They'll be alright. According to the telegram they already have a crew working on it. The train was still in Dodge City."

Hannah moved a rug so Sarah could mop. "Cora, your brother-in-law looked tired at supper last night. I hope they made it home safely."

"I hope so, too. Those dirt roads would have been quagmires. I'm sure he was exhausted. He came in early yesterday, and Mother kept the three little ones while he and Anthony went to the livestock sale. It's not easy to corral four children and run a ranch at the same time. My mother kept Charlie for his first year after Ella died, but when he turned one, Cliff insisted it was time to take him to the ranch. A neighbor girl comes during the day when he works in the fields.

"He seems to be doing a good job with them," Cora continued. "They're always clean, and they seem to be happy. Although it must be frustrating for him at times, he seems to have a handle on it." Cora perched on the edge of the nearest stool. "Anthony's a good worker. Esther, on the other hand, would rather curl up and read a book than help around the house. Cliff has to push her a bit."

"Esther sounds like me when I was that age." Tessa straightened a pile of napkins under the counter of her section. "I'm the oldest in my family, so my mom expected me to help with housework and cooking. I didn't like it much, either. I'd often hide and read a book." She walked around and sat on the stool beside Cora. "I was impressed with the way Cliff interacted with the children. He wasn't impatient with them."

"That's one thing about Cliff. He's a patient man. Not very many men could do what he's done."

Tessa sighed. "My little sisters and brother are about Esther, Anna, and Charlie's age. Kinda' makes me homesick."

A FEW MORNINGS LATER, Tessa threw back the sheet on her bed and sat up. It was almost seven o'clock and the sun was well up in the sky. Hannah's bed was empty. Tessa jumped up as concern coursed through her. Was she late for work? It took her a few moments to get her bearings, then she sighed with relief. It was Sunday morning. She didn't have to work.

She was still trying to catch her breath when Hannah

walked in with a pitcher of water. "Can you believe we slept so late? I usually wake up long before this, even on Sunday."

Tessa chuckled. "It scared me when I saw your empty bed. I thought I was late for work." She took the pitcher Hannah offered and poured water into the bowl on her dresser. A warm breeze blew in the open window. "It looks like the rain's over and the summer heat's returned. The cool weather didn't last long." She splashed her face. The lukewarm water refreshed and awakened her.

Hannah ran her brush through her hair. "Do you want to go to church with us this morning?"

Tessa sat back down on the bed. "Yes, I would. What time do we need to leave?"

"Several of us go with Cora to the church her family attends. It's only four blocks away so we walk together. We meet with the others at ten. Let's get breakfast and then come back and get ready."

Tessa nodded as she padded on bare feet to the wardrobe to get out her Sunday dress. "It's nice to wear something besides a waitress uniform."

"I agree. It's also good to relax for a few hours. This was a busy week." Hannah washed her face and combed her hair, twisting it into a chignon on the back of her head.

Tessa grimaced. "Was this a typical weekend here? We were busy in Topeka, but the schedules were more consistent. We didn't have trains arriving at all hours as Hutchinson does."

"When I first came here to work it confused me, too. You'll get used to it."

"I hope so."

A short while later, they walked down the stairs to the lunchroom. Mary and Susan, Harvey Girls who worked in the dining room, were already sitting at the counter. Tessa and

Hannah joined them. Sarah approached to serve them. "What can I get you, girls, to drink?"

"I'll take coffee with two sugar cubes." Tessa indicated her cup as Sarah turned it over. "Is this your Sunday to work?"

"Yes, Carrie and I are here today. We work one Sunday morning a month. Trains don't run today, but we still have hotel guests and local citizens who come for lunch. Cora will work you into the schedule."

Just then, Maxine and Lucy strolled in with some of the other Harvey House dining-room girls. "Looks like a good group for church this morning." Maxine slid onto the stool.

After the girls finished their breakfasts, they headed to their rooms. Tessa slipped on her dove grey Sunday dress. It fell in graceful folds over her bustle. Then she finished styling her hair and put on her fashionable straw hat adorned with a dark blue ribbon. At nine-forty-five, she and Hannah went down the stairs where the other girls had begun to gather. The sun shone brightly as they left the Harvey House. It was precisely ten o'clock.

"Shall we walk up Main Street or on Walnut?" Cora waved her arm in that general direction.

"Let's go on Main so we can show Tessa the stores." Hannah started down the porch steps. Tessa followed her off the porch and across the tracks. As they walked the three blocks to Sherman Street, Hannah pointed out Blubaugh's Mercantile and Dixon's clothing store. There was another hotel and a doctor's office. She pointed to a small store with an elegant gown in the window. "That's Betty's Dress Shop and Milliner. She's an excellent seamstress, and she designs all her hats. We love browsing there when we have a chance."

As they passed First Street, Maxine pointed to the left. "There's the Post Office one block east. We go by it when we take Walnut Street."

Tessa noticed Perkins General Store and Food Market on the right as they turned East.

"There's our church," Lucy pointed. "Look, Cora, Cliff, and the kids just drove into the parking lot."

Tessa noticed immediately that the white clapboard building was similar to her family's church back home. A steeple reached toward the heavens. She watched Cliff guide the horse and carriage until it moved out of sight behind the building. Her heart went out to the handsome rancher. Raising four active children wasn't an easy task, even with two to share the responsibilities.

As Tessa and the other girls approached the church, Cliff appeared around the side of the building with Charlie on his hip. Her breath caught in her throat. He was stunning! He wore a buff-colored Stetson and his chocolate brown hair brushed the collar of his white shirt. Where he had rolled up his sleeves, his arms were tanned. Denim jeans fit his well-shaped legs and complimented his boots. He looked more rested than the first time she'd seen him. His nut-brown eyes sparkled with humor as he stopped to watch the bevy of girls headed toward him.

Hand-in-hand, Esther and Anna walked sedately, behind their daddy until they spied the Harvey House girls. "Aunt Cora, Aunt Cora," Esther broke into a run and pulled Anna along with her. She dropped Anna's hand and wrapped her arms around Cora. "I'm so glad to see you."

Anna hugged Cora's leg. "I *wuv* you, Aunt Cora."

Tessa grinned as she watched the scene. Esther's hair, chocolate brown like her father's, fell to her shoulders in unruly waves. Tessa's fingers itched to plait it into braids. Esther, at about age eight, was in a rather awkward age--not a small child, but also not a young lady. She pulled away from her aunt and said hello to Tessa. Cora leaned down, picked up Anna, and gave her a squeeze and a kiss.

Anna's angelic face was crowned with curly blonde hair which grew with careless abandon. Both girls wore cotton print dresses and were clean and well cared for, but Tessa noted sadly they lacked the little soft frilly touches a mother would add.

Tessa leaned down to Esther. "Hello, my name's Tessa. I'm a new Harvey Girl here. I saw you in the lunchroom the other evening. You're a beautiful girl. I'd like to get acquainted."

Esther gave her a shy smile. "My name's Esther." She held out her hand. "Can I sit by you?"

Tessa took the offered hand. "You can sit by me if it's alright with your father."

They proceeded toward the front door of the church.

Esther ran to Cliff. "Daddy, this is Tessa. She's a new Harvey Girl. She said I could sit with her if it's okay with you."

Cliff studied Tessa. "I don't believe I've made your acquaintance. My name's Cliff McNance."

"I'm Tessa Gillespie. I just arrived here on Thursday."

Cora stepped up. "She's our newest Harvey Girl."

Cliff glanced at Esther then looked back at Tessa. "Are you sure you want her to sit by you? She's quite a wiggle-worm."

Tessa put her hand on Esther's shoulder. "Yes. We'll be fine. She is a lot like my little sister, Lucile."

Cliff's face became stern as he faced Esther. "You better sit still or next time you'll sit by me. And, you need to address her as Miss Tessa."

Esther took Tessa's hand. "Yes, sir, I'll be good." She walked close to Tessa as they entered the church building and followed the others to a pew near the front. Cliff and Cora carried Anna and Charlie and sat beside an older man and woman on the pew behind them.

Esther snuggled close to Tessa. Her whisper reached Tessa's ear. "I like you, Miss Tessa."

Tessa leaned down. "I like you, too."

Cliff stared at the back of the woman who had so easily won his daughter's heart and confidence. Had she said her name was Tessa? He couldn't remember the last name. The vision of her on the lunchroom stool beside Esther at the Harvey House played in his mind.

He'd been surprised when he walked around the corner of the church and saw her with the other Harvey Girls. Her blonde hair pulled up neatly into a bun on the back of her head, gleamed in the morning sun. Kindness radiated from her beautiful deep brown eyes, especially when she leaned over and responded to Esther. Whatever she said made his little girl beam with happiness.

Lord, could this be the woman you've picked to be my help-mate? He immediately discounted the thought. According to Cora, to be a Harvey Girl, she had to sign a contract not to marry for a year. He didn't want to wait that long. His heart ached and loneliness blanketed him. *God, you know I need a wife. Not just to care for the kids. I need someone to love,* he mused as they all took their seats on the wooden pews in the simple little church.

His friend, Paul Johnson, walked to the pulpit and announced the first song, "At the Cross." Cliff pulled his thoughts back to the present and opened the hymn book. Charlie crawled onto his grandma's lap. Cliff stood with the other worshippers to sing. As the first notes rang out, he heard Tessa's clear soprano voice in front of him declare the beloved words.

SENSING LONELINESS in the little girl beside her, Tessa ached to put her arm around Esther's shoulders and pull her close as they sang the beautiful hymn. Charlie and Anna were still of that innocent age that was easy to love. They often drew the attention and care of those around them. Esther needed attention and love, too.

Tessa felt a kinship with her. When she was about Esther's age, her mother had severely injured her back in a fall. Although her mother was still in her life, Tessa had had to step up and take a lot of the responsibility for cooking, cleaning, and caring for her younger siblings. She was sure Esther had a lot of expectations placed on her, too. Tessa was acutely aware of Cliff standing behind her. What was he thinking? Did he think she had been too assertive to chat casually with his Esther?

The music director announced the next song, "Oh How I Love Jesus." Tessa turned to the page in her hymnal and held it for Esther to see. Then, knowing the words by heart, Tessa lost herself in the beautiful hymn. She did love Jesus with all her heart.

As the song ended and the congregation was seated, a middle-aged man walked to the podium. "Today, our message is from First John chapter four, verses ten through twelve. Let's all read together. *'Herein is love, not that we loved God, but that He loved us, and sent His Son to be the propitiation for our sins. Beloved, if God so loved us, we ought also to love one another. No man hath seen God at any time. If we love one another, God dwelleth in us, and His love is perfected in us.'*

He continued, "God the Father showed His love for us by sending His Son, Jesus, to die for our sins. We show our love for God by loving each other. When we allow God's love to flow through us to others they see God in us. Since no man can see God with their physical eyes, the only way they will see Him is through our love for each other."

The pastor's words burned into Tessa's heart. *Lord, I pray Your love will shine through me to those around me. I want them to know You because of my love.* She put her arm around Esther's shoulder and gave her a little squeeze then listened intently as the pastor expounded on ways to show God's love to others.

When the sermon ended and they stood for the final hymn, Tessa patted Esther on her shoulder. Despite a few fidgets, the little girl had sat quietly during the message.

Cora introduced Tessa to her parents, William and Mildred Dickenson, Cliff's in-laws. Cora smiled at Esther. "You sat very still, today, and listened. I'm proud of you."

Esther faced her father. "Daddy, can I sit by Miss Tessa next Sunday since I sat still today?"

Cliff gazed at Tessa. "I guess she can if it's okay with you. You must have a magic touch. I don't recall that she ever sat that still."

Tessa smiled. "It's fine with me. I love kids and yours have charmed me." She felt the heat rise in her cheeks. Maybe she was too forward.

CHAPTER 3

The Harvey House was abuzz with excitement and anticipation. Tessa wiped the lunch counter and checked to make sure all the supplies were refilled. It was the Fourth-of-July evening. No trains were scheduled to arrive. This was one of the few times throughout the year that the Harvey House was closed for a few hours so the whole crew could attend the celebration at the fairgrounds.

Tessa looked around. "I think we're done. Come on, girls, let's change clothes. I'm *so* ready to go. I haven't been to a carnival since I was fifteen when one came to our town in Arkansas." Tessa, Hannah, Sarah, and Lucy hurried from the lunchroom and up the stairs.

When they reached their room, Tessa untied her apron and stepped out of her uniform. "It'll be exciting to wear normal clothes for the evening." She washed her face and patted it dry then turned to remove her blue flowered dress and her hat from the wardrobe. When she had the bustle tied around her waist, she lifted the dress and slipped it over her head. The gathered ruffles fell over the bustle. "Hannah, will you fasten my bodice then I'll help you?"

"Sure, I'll be glad to. Turn around." Hannah buttoned the dress and straightened the flounce. "You look beautiful. The color enhances your blonde hair."

Tessa looked in the mirror. The lace along the neckline and around the sleeves added to the feminine look. She replaced some hairpins to capture a few errant curls and settled her hat on her head. Then she put some coins in her handbag. She turned back toward Hannah. "I received forty cents in tips this week. It's rewarding to have money to spend."

When Hannah had her dress on, Tessa assisted her. "You look charming, too. Now let's go have some fun."

They met the other girls in the hall, and they all arrived in the lobby. Other staff members were gathered there.

Hannah nudged Tessa and pointed toward a group of railroad workers on the other side of the room. "There's Ben. He's an engine mechanic. I met him at one of our socials. I would like to have him as my beau."

"We've signed a contract not to marry for a year." Tessa frowned.

"I've worked for five months. It wouldn't hurt to begin a relationship."

"In Topeka, I went to a couple of activities with a young man named Edward." Tessa paused in contemplation. "He wants to come to see me here, but I don't want to encourage a serious relationship with anyone." The image of a handsome rancher with four children crossed Tessa's mind, but the next instant she dismissed it. With her contract that couldn't be a consideration.

Cora's voice caught Tessa's attention. "Alright, everyone, we have carriages to take you to the fairgrounds. Let's load."

Tessa started across the room as a young man approached Hannah. "Hello, my name's Ben Masters. You're Miss Johnson, aren't you? I believe we met at the dance, here. Would you accompany me to the celebration in my carriage? Your friend could come along and my co-worker, Paul White, could escort her."

"I'd be pleased to go." Hannah turned toward Tessa. "Do you want to go with Mr. Masters and his friend?"

Tessa shook her head. "Cora expects us to ride in the provided carriages. I'd rather do that." She glanced at Sarah. "Would you like to go with Hannah?"

"Sure." Sarah stepped toward Hannah. "I'll ride with you."

Tessa sighed with relief as she moved across the room toward the door. She didn't need to be seen with another young man. Edward's desire to come to see her was enough to worry about.

The image of Cliff McNance holding little Charlie flashed through her mind. Now there was a real man, lean and muscular, bronzed by the sun. She shook her head. What a silly thought. He had to be more than ten years older than her.

She stepped out to the porch and waited as the next surrey pulled up on the street.

Cora was writing the names of the occupants of each conveyance. She touched Tessa's arm. "Why don't you wait and go with me. I'll show you around and introduce you to some of our citizens."

"Thank you. I'd appreciate that. I was wondering how I'd know where to go." Tessa moved out of line and stood by Cora. She watched Hannah and Sarah wave gaily as they set out with their young men.

When all the Harvey House staff had boarded the carriages, and been accounted for, Cora turned to Tessa. "There's room for us on that last one. Let's go."

The main streets were quiet as they drove through town. Most of the usual Saturday evening shoppers were probably at the Fourth of July celebration. Beautiful, multi-storied houses lined the brick street as they drove down First Avenue, through the residential area to Plum Street, and then south. Before long, they pulled up to the fairgrounds. Colorful tents and tables were set up on each side of a wooden walkway. Wooden bleachers faced a large oval racetrack, and a jumble of children played a game of Red Rover on the grassy area inside the track.

Cora alighted from the carriage. "Come on, let's go find our church's booth. My mom made fried meat pies. They're my favorite."

Tessa followed her through the crowds of townspeople. Lines had formed at several of the tents.

Cora took Tessa's hand and pulled her off the walkway toward the back of a red and blue striped enclosure. "We don't have to stand in line." She ducked through the opening and Tessa followed. Four women bustled about. Two were behind a table at the front of the tent which was loaded with delicious smelling meat and fruit pies. A line of customers filed by and chose their favorites then paid and moved on.

Mrs. Dickenson gathered a handful of pies from a pan on another table and carried them to the front. "Here's more, Bessie. These beef pies seem to be the favorite." She glanced up as she turned, then hurried to Cora and hugged her. "I wondered when you'd get here. I haven't seen Cliff and the children yet. I suppose he had to feed and milk the cows before they could get away."

She turned to Tessa with a smile. "Hi, Tessa, right? It's good to see you again." She gestured toward the table. "Pick out what you want. We have beef, chicken, and pork meat pies and cherry, apricot, and apple fruit pies."

The tantalizing aromas hovered in the air. Tessa's stomach rumbled. She giggled as she grasped her middle. "I guess I'm hungrier than I realized. I'll take pork and apricot. My folks have an apricot tree. I love them." She handed Cora's mom two nickels in exchange for the pies.

Cora chose beef and apple. "Thanks, Mom. We'll go sit outside and watch for Cliff and the kids."

Outside, they sat at a nearby table and ate the meat pies.

Tessa pointed. "There's the water barrel. Does your mom have a clean dipper? I'm thirsty."

"Yes, I'm sure she does. She always brings one so we don't have to drink after everyone else." Cora glanced around. "Did you see the Harvey House booth? Henry, our baker, made dozens of cookies, and they have lemonade. Would you rather have that? They brought the tin cups we use when we have picnics."

"Lemonade sounds wonderful."

"I didn't see them when we came in, but let's go find them. They're probably farther down."

They soon found the Harvey House booth. John, one of the cooks' helpers, poured cups of cold lemonade and sat them on the table. "Don't forget to bring your cups back. George will wash them so we can reuse them."

Cora headed to the table where Sam handed out cookies. "Looks like you're busy. Can I have an oatmeal cookie?"

"You sure can, ma'am. Yes, it's been busy. A couple of the guys came out and set up, then we came after supper. William and James will come as soon as they finish cleaning the kitchen."

Cora nodded and turned to Tessa. "What do you want, Tessa? Have you met Sam? He's our head cook."

"I'm glad to meet you. I'd like a sugar cookie and a cup of lemonade."

Sam handed them to her. "You girls having a good time?"

Cora nodded. "We haven't been here long. I waited until everyone was loaded and accounted for."

As they returned, Carrie, Maxine, Lucy, and some of the other girls from the Harvey House walked toward them. Carrie and Lucy each had a piece of fried chicken.

"Hey, where did you get the fried pies? Those look good." Maxine stopped by the table where Cora and Tessa were.

"In there." Cora pointed toward the nearby tent. "The Baptist Ladies Missionary Society is selling them. My mom's in charge."

Lucy pointed across the walkway. "The Methodist Church is having a cakewalk. Maybe we can win a cake to share."

"The Harvey House booth is farther down. We'll have to go say, hi. I also saw watermelon." Carrie sat at the table to eat her chicken. "There's so much good food. I'll eat too much if I'm not careful."

Tessa listened to the chatter among these new friends. She sighed happily, realizing she was glad she'd been transferred to this Harvey House.

"Look, there comes Mr. McNance." Lucy gave a dramatic sigh. "He's so handsome. It makes me wish I hadn't signed that contract."

Just then, Maxine returned with two fried pies and settled next to Lucy. She scrunched her nose. "You ready to take on four kids? Not me! No matter how good-looking he is."

Tessa's pulse quickened as she saw the little family approach. Her eyes were on Cliff as he strode toward their table. He was the epitome of vital manhood, tall, and tanned. His cotton shirt failed to disguise the rippling muscles in his arms as he shifted Charlie on his hip. Her cheeks grew warm as he caught her eye and smiled. She averted her gaze as heat flooded her cheeks, appalled that she'd been caught staring shamelessly.

"Daddy, there's Aunt Cora and Miss Tessa." Tessa glanced

up when she heard her name. Esther was holding Anna's hand and run-walking to keep up with Cliff.

"I see them. And, this is our church's food tent. I'm sure your grandma's in there."

Esther dropped Anna's hand and ran toward Cora. She threw her arms around her aunt. "Hi. I've been so excited to come. I didn't think Daddy would ever get ready. We're gonna hear some music then see fireworks." She turned back to her dad. "Can I go play Red Rover out on the track? All the other kids are out there."

Cliff shook his head no as he set Charlie on the bench beside Cora. Anna grabbed his leg. "Hold me."

He looked down at her. "No, Anna. You have all these girls to hold you. I have to get something to eat."

"Where's Anthony?" Cora unwrapped Anna's arms from Cliff's leg and lifted her onto her lap. Anna puckered her face to cry, but Cora tickled her, and she giggled. Carrie gathered up Charlie and held him.

"He found the Jackson boys and went to talk to them."

"Daddy, can I go play Red Rover?"

"No, Esther, I told you we had to eat first. You can't go if you don't eat at least half of a meat pie. You can share one with Anna."

Esther pushed out her lower lip. "I'm not hungry. I wanna go and play."

Cliff gave her a stern look. "You can't play if you don't eat. You'll be hungry later." He turned and walked toward the church tent.

Tessa reached out to Esther. "Come here and sit by me. If you eat your fried pie and it's okay with your daddy, I'll walk to the track with you. Would you like that?"

Esther frowned, but she nodded.

"While we're waiting, I think I'll get some watermelon.

Would you like a piece after you eat your pie?" Tessa put her arm around Esther.

"Yes." Esther nodded again.

"How about you, Cora, Carrie, would you like some?"

At their nods, Tessa stood and patted Esther's back. "You stay here with Aunt Cora, and I'll be back."

Tessa, Maxine, and Lucy walked around the ring of booths. There were many delicacies: fried chicken, baked goods, bread, cinnamon rolls, fruit pies, cakes, pulled taffy, and popcorn. The German Mennonite table featured sauerkraut and homemade sausage.

"Yum, everything looks and smells so good, but I'm hungry for watermelon." Tessa pointed. "Here's what we're looking for."

The three girls gathered enough slices for everyone. Tessa pulled out her coin purse. "That's seven slices so we owe you fourteen cents. Here's a dime for five of them." Maxine and Lucy paid for their own.

When they got back to their table, Cliff had returned and Esther and Anna were each eating a meat pie. Tessa set the watermelon on the table. "Here, we got everyone a slice. We'll have to eat it over the grass, though, so we don't get juice everywhere, especially on our clothes."

Cliff pointed to Esther and raised his eyebrows. "I don't know what you told her, but it worked. I had to go get another one for me."

"I just told her if she ate her pie, she could have some watermelon. And that I would walk with her to the track if that's okay with you."

He raised his eyebrows and nodded. "Sounds good, if you want to."

By the time Tessa was ready, Esther had consumed her pie and watermelon and stood waiting. Cora borrowed a towel from her mother and they washed their hands and faces with water from the water barrel.

"Okay, let's go." Tessa took Esther's hand and they strolled together to the edge of the track. "You go play. I'll sit on the bleachers and watch." As Esther ran to get in the game with her friends, Tessa marveled at how quickly this little girl--so much like herself a few years ago--had stolen her heart.

Tessa smoothed the front of her dress. Thankfully, she hadn't soiled it with watermelon juice. She found a seat on the bleachers and watched the children play. Two women supervised the games; Duck, Duck, Goose, and a lively game of Hot Potato. Tessa smiled. One of the ladies sang as they passed the knotted cloth around the circle.

Local band members set up chairs on the racetrack in preparation for the concert. Anthony and several other boys his age traipsed across the grass and behind the bleachers. No telling what mischief they'd find to do.

Tessa's breath caught in her throat as Cliff appeared at the end of the bleachers. He held Anna's hand and Charlie sat on his shoulders. Tessa smiled as Charlie yelled, "Giddy up." He bounced up and down and waved his arms in the air.

Cliff ambled toward her. He lowered Charlie to the ground then stepped into the bleachers. Tessa's heart stopped, then went full gallop, as he sat beside her. She was vitally aware of his masculinity and the outdoorsy aroma that emanated from him. An errant lock of hair had escaped his broad-brimmed hat and fell across his forehead. Charlie and Anna started to play in the grass.

"Thank you for taking an interest in my Esther." His rich voice resonated through Tessa. "She's been my challenge. She's strong-willed and doesn't want to obey. Of all the kids, Esther's taken the loss of Ella the hardest. She was six when her mama died, right when she needed her most. You have connected with her somehow."

"When I was her age, my mother injured her back in a fall and was bedridden for several months. After she got up and about, she couldn't do a lot. The responsibility for cleaning, cooking, and taking care of my siblings fell on me. I didn't lose her, but I had to grow up quickly." Tessa shrugged. "I feel a kinship with Esther and wanted to encourage her. She's a sweet girl."

"Yes, she is. And she is an immense help with the two little ones. Maybe I expect too much of her. I do have Wanda, the neighbor girl, come in to help when I have to work or be away during the day."

"It's natural to expect her to help," Tessa encouraged him. "I think, from what I've seen, that you're a wonderful father. The kids are all well-mannered and obedient. I find them a joy to be around."

Cliff laughed. "You obviously don't see the whole picture." He gazed at Anna and Charlie who were giggling and busily exploring near them.

"Look, Daddy." Anna climbed up beside them. "A roly-poly." She opened her chubby little hand and showed him her treasure.

"A roly-poly." Charlie clambered up beside her and opened his hand to show the little ball on his palm.

"Yes, I see. They're all rolled up because they're scared. You better put them back so they can be with their family."

Anna frowned and rolled her eyes. "I think he wants to play with me." The roly-poly uncurled and started crawling. Anna touched it, and it rolled back into a ball.

"Okay, but when you're through playing, put him back. I'm sure he wants to be with his family." Anna climbed back down with Charlie close behind her, his little fist clenched tightly.

31

Tessa's heart swelled with admiration for this man who interacted so lovingly with his small children. He'd been thrust into the position of being both father and mother, and, for the most part, the children appeared to thrive.

Cora and the other Harvey Girls filtered up into the stands and found seats around them. The band members had assembled and were tuning their instruments. Esther traipsed off the field with the other children then climbed up and sat beside Tessa, who caught a whiff of a sweaty little girl.

"Did you have a good time?" Tessa put her arm around Esther.

"Yes. I made some new friends and the games were fun."

"I'm glad." Tessa watched Anna and Charlie as they dug in the dirt in front of the stands. It didn't take much to entertain little children.

The sun drifted lazily toward the western horizon and a cooling breeze swirled around them, providing respite from the day's heat. The musicians took their seats and prepared to begin the concert. Tessa smiled at the assortment of instruments represented. There were two violins and a stringed bass; two trumpets, a trombone, a saxophone, and a flute. She noticed that a man who looked to be in his late thirties was guided to stand beside the chairs, a drum strapped to his side.

Cliff leaned toward her. "The man they just escorted onto the track is Chester White. He was a drummer boy during the Civil War and was blinded in one of the battles, but he never stopped playing. He always performs with the band. The lead trumpeter was a bugler during the war."

Tessa watched Chester and tried to imagine what it must have been like to be in the battle as a teenager and suddenly lose your sight.

The band director stepped forward. "Could I have your attention?" The chatter grew quiet. "We welcome you to the

Fourth of July celebration. We'll begin by playing "Amazing Grace," then we'll play the patriotic songs: "America", "America the Beautiful", "Battle Hymn of the Republic", and "The Star-Spangled Banner." Everyone please stand and salute the flag when we play our national anthem."

To Tessa's delight, the band was excellent. It was obvious they'd spent a lot of time practicing. The beautiful songs, which celebrated the United States, flowed around her. She was proud she lived in America.

Anna and Charlie finally climbed up into the seats. Cora lifted Charlie onto her lap, and Anna tugged on Cliff's pant leg.

Tessa held out her hand to Anna. "Come sit on my lap. I'll hold you."

After glancing up at her daddy, Anna scooted toward Tessa. She snuggled down on Tessa's lap and yawned.

It must be past her bedtime. Tessa relished the cuddles of the little girl. Her youngest sister, Betsy, was the same age as Anna. A longing to see her family swept over Tessa as she hugged this little one. Her mother hadn't been able to do much work around the house, but that hadn't hindered her from having babies. After Tessa's five sisters, Margaret, Abigail, Theresa, Lucile, and Betsy, she'd finally had a boy, Samuel. Tessa had become an expert tending to babies. Despite the responsibilities she'd carried, she loved and missed them all, intensely.

She stood with Anna in her arms when the band played *the Star-Spangled Banner.* She was proud to salute the American flag, with its 38 stars, and to be a part of this celebration. As the song ended, a show of fireworks lit up the night sky with rockets, wheels, serpents, fountains, and sunflowers. She smiled at the exclamations of "oh, "wow," "beautiful" which surrounded her. It was exciting to be with her friends, and this little family, to celebrate the birth of their nation.

Cliff stood beside Tessa and saluted the flag. It seemed so natural to have her beside him holding his daughter. He watched her enraptured face as she stood engrossed in the fireworks display. Why did she have to sign a year contract with Fred Harvey? On the other hand, if she hadn't, she wouldn't even be here. Frustration shot through him. Here she was, maybe the perfect woman for him and his children, and she wasn't available.

At the end of the show, Tessa untangled Anna and handed her off to him. "She's so sleepy. I don't think she'll stay awake until you get out of the parking lot."

He nodded. "I thought that might be the case. I put a blanket in the back of the carriage. Both she and Charlie will probably sleep all the way home." He stepped down from the bleachers then turned to offer her his help. Her touch sent fireworks up his arm as she accepted his assistance. He didn't want to release her hand. She gazed at him then pulled slowly away. Had she felt the connection?

"Thank you. This has been a delightful evening." Tessa nodded to him then turned and hugged Esther. "I'm happy I spent it with you."

Esther shuffled her toe in the dirt. "Thank you for watching me play."

"I enjoyed watching you with your friends. You run fast."

Cliff watched Tessa as she joined the other Harvey Girls, and walked out of the fairgrounds. Then he turned and scanned the bleachers for Anthony. He spied him still at the top, laughing and talking with his friends. He was glad Anthony could spend this evening with his buddies. They didn't get together often. He caught his son's eye and motioned him down. His voice carried up, "Come on, it's time to go. Meet me at the carriage."

Cliff walked with Cora and Esther. Cora held Charlie, who was asleep, his head nestled on her shoulder. "What happens if a Harvey Girl decides to break her contract?"

Cora stopped and turned toward him. "What are you saying?" She scowled at him. "Why do you ask that?"

"Oh, I don't know. I was just wondering."

"Don't you get any ideas! I know you want a wife, but these girls sought employment with Fred Harvey for a reason. Some send money to their families back home; some want adventure or travel. If they quit before their contract is complete, they lose their salary, the privilege to travel on the Santa Fe free of charge, their room and board, and all the benefits that accompany their positions. There are very few jobs for working women with prestige and decent money."

"Okay, okay. It was just a simple question." Cliff raised his free hand. "Now I know."

Cora turned and walked with purpose toward the parking lot. "I need to get to the Harvey House vehicles to make sure everyone's there." She laid Charlie on the blanket in the back of Cliff's carriage. "I'll see you Sunday, if not before."

"I was only curious," Cliff mumbled in defense, as he watched Cora stride across the lot. He was foolish to even consider that Tessa might be interested in him. She was young and carefree. Besides, she had practically raised her siblings. Not likely she'd want to take on four children who weren't in the slightest related to her.

CORA AND TESSA rode side-by-side in the carriage, back to the Harvey House. Tessa put her hand to her chest. Her fingers tingled from the warmth of Cliff's touch as he helped her off the bleachers. Her startled reaction surprised her. He was the most fascinating man she'd ever met, but a romantic attraction between them was premature...wasn't it? She'd been drawn to his children because of the bond she missed with the little ones back home. Someone closer to his age would probably attract him more. Besides, she had to fulfill her Harvey Girl contract. Right?

CHAPTER 4

Tessa dangled her legs off the side of her bed and stared out the window. The sky had spread its light in the east and a cool breeze wafted through the window. Today, the fifteenth of July, was her twentieth birthday. A lump of pain settled in her chest. Almost two months had passed since she'd seen her family.

Until the day she left for her interview in Kansas City, she'd slept every night with her younger sisters. They'd laughed together and discussed the events of their day. Since she became a Harvey Girl, she'd grown accustomed to sleeping by herself, but this morning she missed the camaraderie of home. She reached under her pillow and pulled out the letter from her mother. It'd arrived two days ago and she'd read it at least a dozen times. Everything seemed alright at home. All her siblings had signed the paper even down to Betsy and Samuel, though it was obvious Samuel had to have help. It made her teary to see their childish scrawls, the largest names on the page.

Hannah rolled over and squinted at her through the semi-darkness. "What time is it?"

"Almost five-thirty. We need to get ready for work."

Hannah pushed back her sheet and sat up. "Why are you awake so early? I'm usually the early bird."

"I'm missing my family." Tessa waved the letter. "How do you stand it being away from home for so long?"

"I know it's not easy. I've almost earned my six-month visit. I can hardly wait to see my family. Our farm in Pennsylvania is a long way from Hutchinson. It seems like forever since I've seen them."

Tessa stood and placed the letter on her dresser. "I'm only a third of the way there, but I'll make it."

"The time goes by faster than you'd think. We're so busy there isn't a lot of time to think about it." Hannah yawned and stretched her arms over her head.

"That's for sure. There are *always* railroad crews to feed, with freight trains in and out at all hours."

"Especially now with wheat threshing in full swing. The farmers are shipping their grain. And ranchers are moving steers and calves before the heat dries the grass."

Tessa picked up the pitcher from the dresser set. "I'll get some fresh water." She strolled out the door and down the hall to the water closet. She used the commode, then filled the pitcher from the reservoir over the metal bathtub--a real luxury.

Hannah was combing her hair when Tessa returned. She turned toward Tessa. "I'm so sorry. I forgot today was your birthday. No wonder you missed your family. We need to have a party."

Tessa laughed. "That's not necessary. I'm alright now." She washed her face and prepared for work.

The morning sped by. After breakfast, Tessa watched the last of her customers leave the lunchroom. She gathered the dirty dishes and carried them to the dish room. Would Cliff be in soon? She'd seen him briefly at church on Sunday, but there was no chance to talk. She took the dishcloth and headed back to clean her station.

Cora walked in with several envelopes. "Tessa, you have two letters today. Someone must have known it was your birthday." She laid them on the counter.

Excitement rushed through Tessa as she glimpsed the return address on the top one. It was from her friend, Elise Dumond. The other was from Edward. She grimaced. She'd hoped he'd forget to contact her. He was nice enough, and she'd had fun with him at the Harvey Girl activities in Topeka. But she only wanted to be friends with him. She shoved the letters together, slipped them into her pocket, and finished wiping the counter.

After Cora distributed the other letters, she sat on the stool by Tessa's station. "I've been so busy this morning I haven't had an opportunity to wish you a happy birthday. We'll have a cake after dinner. Why don't you take a break when you're finished and read your letters."

"Thank you. I'd like that."

"By the way, next Monday, we'll plan for you to serve a meal to Mr. McKinsey and me. I think you're ready and I want to work you into the dining room schedule."

Tessa nodded. "Okay." Nervous flutters filled her midsection. "I'm probably as ready as I'll ever be."

Cora smiled. "It's intimidating, but you'll do fine. It's not as frightening as it sounds." She stood and walked from the lunchroom.

Tessa returned the cleaning cloth to the dish room, hurried from the lunchroom, and made her way up the stairs. She pulled the envelopes from her pocket as she hustled through the parlor to her room. She ran her finger under the seal on Elise's letter, sat on her bed, and pulled out the written page.

July 13, 1885

Dear Tessa,

How is your new House? I like the one in Emporia and what I've seen in the town. The girls here are friendly and encouraging. I had quite an experience on the Fourth of July. Rosa, my roommate, insisted I accompany her and her beau to the dance and fireworks display. They were late getting back to the house. I thought I was a goner, but Rosa got us in without being detected. I was scared to death I'd be sent home. Rosa has since been fired by Fred Harvey for wearing make-up. I tell you, I'll not break the rules ever again if I can help it! I have a new roommate, but no one can take your place. You'll always be my special friend.

I miss Daniel so much. Of course, I haven't heard a word from him since the one letter when he left. I hope he'll want to be with me when he returns. It's hard to wait. Have you heard from Edward? I think he likes you.

It's turned off hot and dry here after the rain when I first arrived. Can you believe we've worked for almost two months? We'll soon receive our first pay. I'm eager to send money home to help with the farm payment.

I hope you've made good friends and have a good group of girls to work with. Please write and let me know how you are.

Your friend,

Elise

Tessa held the letter to her heart, grateful it had arrived on her birthday, then laid it beside her on the bed. She'd already made friends here in Hutchinson, but none compared to the bond she and Elise had.

What was in Edward's letter? She'd enjoyed the time she spent with him at the socials in Topeka, but that was behind her. The vision of Cliff's handsome face and his love and concern for his family came to mind. Edward was attractive and thoughtful, but he didn't inspire her strong feelings. She tore open the envelope.

Dear Tessa,

I wanted to let you know that I enjoyed making your acquaintance in Topeka. I asked Miss Peterson where you'd moved and she gave me your address.

I've been transferred to another station in New Mexico so I'll travel through Hutchinson on Friday, the twenty-fourth of July. I'd like to see you if possible. The train schedule puts me in there about six o'clock. Please let me know if that's acceptable.

Your friend,

Edward Davis

Tessa wrinkled her nose. He would be here and there wasn't anything to do about it. Hopefully, Cora and the other girls wouldn't think they were a couple. She didn't need that kind of gossip to complicate her friendship with Cliff. She refolded the note, slipped it back into the envelope, and laid it on the dresser. Then she pushed Elise's letter in her pocket and returned to work. It was time to prepare for the noon rush.

"Did you get good news?" Carrie placed a pile of clean napkins under the counter as Tessa returned.

"I did. They were from my friends. The best one was from my former roommate, Elise Dumond. It was a joy to hear from her. We met at our interview and became close friends. She was transferred to Emporia when I came here." Tessa patted her pocket. She stepped to her station and arranged the napkins and silverware in front of her stools in preparation for the new train passengers.

Her seats were soon filled and she began the routine of serving her customers. As they finished their desserts, Tessa's breath caught in her throat. Cliff's familiar voice reached her, over the hum of conversation. She strained to hear his words as he and Cora stepped through the lunchroom door.

"The wheat threshing crew will be at my farm tomorrow morning. I had to come to get some parts for my wagon. I brought Anna and Charlie in to stay with your parents until we're done. It'd be hard for Wanda and Esther to keep an eye on them with all the extra harvest work. Thankfully, Wanda's mom came over to help cook for the crew. She and the girls will serve the meals." He shook his head. "I don't know what I'd do if I didn't have helpful neighbors and my wonderful in-laws."

Cora nodded. "Mom and Dad will enjoy the children. It's too bad Esther couldn't come, too, but I know you need her help."

Tessa watched as Cliff scanned the lunch counter. When their eyes met an instant smile spread across his face. Tessa's heart lurched and she released her breath. She smiled, then turned her attention to her patrons.

As the train passengers stood and left their seats, Cliff sauntered over and sat on one of the stools in her area. "May I sit here?"

"Yes, you may. Let me clear the counter, and I'll get your drink order." Tessa saw Cora frown and stalk from the room.

"That's okay. I'm not in a hurry." Cliff crossed his arms and relaxed against the back of the seat. There was a decided twinkle in his eyes.

Tessa gathered the used dessert plates and carried them to the dish room, then returned to wipe the counter. Her heart beat against her ribs. Why had Cliff chosen to sit at her station? He was so devastatingly handsome! *She shouldn't be attracted to him. She'd just begun her year contract. This was no time for a serious romance of any kind.* She placed a napkin and silverware in front of him. "I heard you say you'll thresh your wheat tomorrow. What's that entail? I grew up on a farm, but my dad raised corn. We had to shuck the ears."

Cliff leaned forward. "Wheat's relatively new to this area. My Mennonite neighbors east of here, around the town of

Buhler, brought good quality grain from Russia. It's planted in the fall and harvested the next summer. I cut it in June and bound it into shocks with a binder. The Mennonites travel from farm to farm with their threshing machine. It separates the grain from the straw. I'll sell some of it and save some for feed." He sighed. "I'm responsible for providing meals for their crew." He grimaced. "I know you probably think I shouldn't make Esther help, but when this is happening, she enjoys being involved."

"Oh, no. I don't feel that way at all. She's old enough to help. I think it sounds fascinating." Tessa laid her cloth aside and handed him a menu. "What can I get you to drink?"

"I'll have an iced tea, no sugar."

The other stools in Tessa's section were filled with local patrons. She angled his cup against the saucer which was a signal of his preference to the girl who served the drinks. Then she moved on to the next customer.

CLIFF PICKED up the menu and studied the selections, then watched Tessa as she moved from customer to customer. She was lovely. He'd been captivated by her charm from the moment he first saw her. *Lord, why am I drawn to a woman who's so out of reach? Please, take this desire away if it's not Your will.* He sent the silent prayer heavenward. He didn't want a wife of convenience to take care of his house and children. He needed someone he could love, and who would love him.

"Have you decided what you want? May I take your order?" Tessa's voice brought him from his reverie. He'd hardly noticed when one of the other girls brought his iced tea.

He focused on Tessa's face. "I'd like the Monte Christo with the French slaw and a piece of cherry pie for dessert."

Hannah leaned over from her station next to Tessa's. "Today's Tessa's birthday. We're gonna have cake when we've finished serving dinner. You better save room for that. I'm sure she wouldn't mind if you stayed."

Cliff studied Tessa, whose cheeks had grown pink. "Happy birthday. By all means, cancel the pie. I'd love a piece of birthday cake."

Tessa smiled demurely and dropped her gaze. "Thank you. I'd like for you to stay and tell me more about threshing." She moved along the counter to take orders.

Before long, she brought his plate. He bowed his head and thanked God for his food then took a bite of the delicious sandwich. The crunch of the crispy french toast coating blended with the turkey, ham, and melted cheese on the inside. The Harvey House food was a welcome reprieve after eating his own cooking.

When Cliff finished his meal, he sat back and considered the activity around him. He should head home. He'd left Anthony to make the last-minute preparations for the threshing. He and his eldest son had worked the last few days cleaning the wooden granaries so they'd be ready for the new crop. When he returned home, he'd still have to repair the wagon and get it ready to hitch up in the morning. The threshers would be there bright and early.

The lunchroom girls efficiently cleaned their stations. As they finished, the head baker led the other cooks and kitchen helpers from the kitchen. He carried a magnificent, three-layer, chocolate cake on a crystal plate. The girls from the dining room trooped in and found seats around the counter as Cora began to sing, "*Happy birthday to you, Happy birthday to you, Happy birthday dear Tessa, Happy birthday to you!*"

Cliff watched Tessa's face while he joined in the song. Though she was embarrassed, he could tell she was pleased. It dawned on him how homesick she must feel to be so far away from home and family on her birthday.

"Thank you so much, Henry! This cake looks heavenly." Tessa accepted the first piece. "And thank you all for your good wishes. It means a lot to share it with my new friends." She reached for the serving spatula.

"Shoo! Go sit down" Hannah waved Tessa out from behind the lunch counter. "We'll serve everyone."

Cliff was gratified that she sat in the empty seat next to him. He wanted to touch her hand but accepted a generous slice of the enticing cake instead. He observed Tessa as she slowly ate her cake. She smiled as she scanned the rest of the staff. How could he think of taking her away from this supportive group to live on a ranch and care for four children who weren't her own? Could she grow to love him? Disappointment overwhelmed him. Despite his desires, he wouldn't settle for a loveless marriage.

He swiveled his stool toward Tessa. "Thanks for including me in your celebration. The cake was delicious. I better go, though. I have a lot to finish before the threshers arrive."

"I'm glad you came in and shared it with me. I'll pray that your threshing goes well."

Cliff stared at her. "You will? You'll pray for us?" His heart pounded. "I appreciate that."

"It's the least I can do. I wish I could help, too. It sounds intriguing."

Cliff chuckled. "It's more like hard work." He slipped off the stool.

Cora walked over. "Are you ready to leave?"

"Yes, I need to get home and prepare for tomorrow. As long as we don't have problems, I'll be back on Friday to pick up the kids." He waved to the others as he strode across the room. He collected his hat from the hook beside the door, placed it on his head, and disappeared into the lobby.

TESSA WATCHED HIS PROGRESS. He moved with confidence. It wasn't fair for a man to be so good-looking and so caring. The essence of the outdoors combined with shaving soap still lingered from him.

When he gazed at her, his expression made her insides flutter. What happened to her resolve not to get involved with a man? She would be thrilled to become better acquainted with Cliff McNance and his children, if only it weren't for the Harvey Girl contract she'd signed. What would Elise say if she knew of Tessa's conflicted feelings? What would Cora say?

She turned back toward her co-workers in the lunchroom. They visited among themselves and enjoyed the brief reprieve from their busy schedule.

CHAPTER 5

The afternoon heat was oppressive in the lunchroom. All the windows were open, but there was no hint of a breeze. Tessa, Hannah, and Maxine sat at the counter and polished silverware, a never-ending job due to Fred Harvey's high standards.

Tessa laid aside the spoon she'd shined then removed a handkerchief from her apron pocket and wiped it across her eyes. "It's beastly hot. I just had sweat running into my eye." She picked up a cardboard fan and waved it in front of her face.

Hannah rubbed a fork with her polishing cloth. "At lunchtime, Cora said the thermometer on the porch read ninety-eight degrees. I bet it's hotter now."

"Whew, that's too hot!" Tessa stood. "I need some ice water. Do you want me to get you each a glass?"

"Please. That would be wonderful, Tessa." Maxine pushed the container of spoons away. "There, finished with those. I'll help you with the water." She stood and followed Tessa to the kitchen. "I heard you served your meal to Mr. McKinsey and Cora on Monday. Will you be working in the dining room next week?"

"Yes, Cora said she'd schedule me there Monday. I'm nervous, but I'm also anticipating it."

"You'll be fine. They wouldn't put you in there unless they knew you were ready."

Tessa nodded. It was hard to believe she'd been in Hutchinson for almost a month. This was Friday, July twenty-fourth. Edward was supposed to be on the evening train. There hadn't been time to answer his letter. He was the first man who had ever shown an interest in her. There weren't many eligible males in her small town in Arkansas.

Since she'd met Cliff, she knew Edward wasn't the one for her. He had the qualities of a good man and a hard worker, but he didn't make her feel alive when she was around him like Cliff did. Even if she couldn't have a relationship with Cliff, she wouldn't settle for less.

She washed her hands, then used the pick to chip pieces of ice from the huge block in the icebox and dropped them in their glasses. "That cool air feels good. I'd like to crawl in there for a while." Tessa smiled at Maxine as she latched the heavy door shut.

Maxine chuckled. "I know, but it'd feel hotter when you got out."

They filled the glasses from the water reservoir. One advantage of working as a Harvey Girl was the availability of fresh spring water and ice brought in on the train. Fred Harvey required that the coffee should taste the same at each Harvey House along the line--another mark of his high standards.

Hannah had finished polishing the forks when Tessa and Maxine returned to the lunchroom. "Let's go sit on the porch. Maybe there'll be a breeze out there."

Tessa scanned the room. Two hotel patrons were sitting at the counter. Carrie was visiting with them as they drank iced tea and ate pie. Lucy was busy polishing the coffee pots and

Sarah was restocking supplies. The evening train would arrive in an hour and a half. "Okay, let's take a break." She motioned to Sarah. "We'll be on the porch. Come out when you're through if you want."

Sarah nodded. "I'm almost done."

The three girls sauntered through the lobby and onto the porch. It was a bit cooler under the shade, and a slight breeze finally began to stir the air.

Tessa settled into one of the deck chairs and drank deeply of the cold water. "Whew! The summer heat has set in. We could use some rain."

"It hasn't rained since that huge gully-washer we got when you arrived." Hannah sighed as she sat in the chair beside her. "The grass has turned brown."

Tessa leaned back and closed her eyes. It felt good to relax. "This is what you should do when it's sweltering. Just sit still and let the warmth seep into your bones. It's too much effort to work."

Carrie laughed. "You're a dreamer. We're Harvey Girls, remember? We're lucky to have a few minutes to drink a glass of water."

"I know, but I can wish."

"Look, Grandma, Miss Tessa's on the porch."

Tessa opened her eyes and sat forward at the sound of Anna's voice. The little girl ran up the steps. Mildred Dickenson followed, holding Charlie's hand.

Anna hurried across the porch to Tessa's chair. "Whatcha' doin'?"

Tessa smiled at her. "We're taking a quick break. It's hotter than the cook's kitchen in the lunchroom."

"It's scorching everywhere." Mrs. Dickenson dabbed a handkerchief to the sweat that gathered on her forehead. "Is Cora inside?" She looked rather frazzled.

"I think she's at the registration desk." Hannah gestured toward the door.

"Grandma, can I sit out here with Miss Tessa?" Anna stood by Tessa's chair.

Mrs. Dickenson peered at Tessa. "Is that alright with you?"

Tessa lifted Anna beside her. "She can sit here for a little while. I have to go back to work soon."

"Then you can stay while I talk to Aunt Cora for a few minutes. I'll be right back." Grandma Dickenson picked up Charlie and shook her head, wearily. "These two 'bout wore me out. They have so much energy."

Tessa smiled. "I know what it's like. I have a little sister and brother about their ages. They're very active, but I miss them terribly. Anna and Charlie help keep my homesickness at bay when they're around."

Anna snuggled next to Tessa and gave a huge yawn as Mrs. Dickenson disappeared inside. Tessa brushed the damp curls out of Anna's eyes. She smiled. The little girl's hair was an unruly mass of blonde ringlets.

Despite the heat, Tessa cherished the pressure of Anna's little body beside her. She leaned down and placed a soft kiss on top of Anna's head as a sweet new love for this precious little one washed through her. Anna was so like Betsy.

Anna looked up with drowsy eyes. "I love you, Miss Tessa."

"Oh, honey, I love you, too."

"Cliff's children have taken up with you." Carrie set her glass on the arm of the chair.

"They sense that I love children, I think. My mother is an invalid so I did most of the housekeeping and childcare. I have five younger sisters and one little brother about Charlie's age." Tessa sighed. "I'm excited to send some money home when I receive my paycheck."

"Next week!" Hannah picked up a cardboard fan from the

table beside her and waved it in front of her face. "Payday's next week, on Thursday."

Sarah joined them on the porch. She chuckled as she pointed at Anna. "She must have been tired. She's fast asleep."

Tessa laughed. "She's been with her grandma for the last couple of days. She probably wore herself out playing." She shifted a bit to watch Anna's even breathing. "Now, how can I go back to work? I guess I'll just have to stay here."

She looked up as Cora and her mother walked back out onto the porch.

Cora smiled. "Well, Tessa. You certainly have the touch. Mom said Anna wouldn't take a nap."

"She finally stopped long enough to relax." Tessa moved her arm to a more comfortable position. "I guess her tiredness caught up with her. I'm sure the sunshine didn't hurt." She sighed. "I'll need to go back to work in a few minutes."

"Here, let me get her. She can sleep on one of the sofas in the lobby until her daddy comes. I can watch her while I work." Cora leaned over and gathered Anna into her arms.

Tessa sat up and finished her water. She could still feel the warmth and dampness of Anna's little body. She stood and shook her apron. "I better go change. My apron is pretty wrinkled. It wouldn't pass inspection."

"It was refreshing to take a break." Hannah and the other girls rose and followed Tessa back into the lunchroom.

When the train arrived an hour later, the girls were prepared and ready at their stations. Tessa watched the door anxiously. What would it be like to see Edward again? It had only been a month since she'd attended the socials with him. So much had happened in the meantime it seemed much longer.

Would Cliff come in while Edward was here? Would he

think she and Edward were a couple? Did it matter? The questions tumbled inside of her head.

Train passengers filtered into the lunchroom. Tessa spied Edward as he conversed with Cora then walked into the room. He wore dark trousers and a white shirt with the sleeves rolled up. A black jacket was folded over his arm. Tessa had to admit to herself that he was quite good-looking with his sandy hair and brown eyes, which lit up when he spotted her at the lunch counter. He headed in her direction and draped his jacket over the back of a swivel chair stool. "Hello, Tessa, it's good to see you again. May I sit here?"

Tessa nodded. "Sit anywhere you like. It's nice to see you again, too." She gestured for him to have a seat. "Did you have a good trip?"

"It was uneventful except for the heat. It was pleasant being a passenger instead of working the rails." He grinned as he took a seat. "I'm glad I don't have to wear this jacket."

Tessa chuckled. "I don't blame you. It's been extremely hot--around a hundred, with no breeze. I think summer's here in full force. We sure could use some rain." Tessa handed him a menu as the other seats at her station filled up. "What would you like to drink?"

"I'd like a large glass of iced tea with sugar. I need something cold."

Tessa angled his cup against the saucer and placed a sugar cube in a small dish near his silverware then took the orders of the others in her section.

She hurried back to the drink station to fill their orders. As she poured tea and water in the different glasses and dropped chunks of ice in them, her mind was a-whirl. How would she tell Edward that she wasn't interested in him, at least not in a romantic way? He was charming and cordial, but there wasn't enough attraction for her to pursue a relationship. Besides, there was the Harvey Girl contract...and there was Cliff McNance! Nothing would likely ever come of that, but poor Edward just didn't measure up when compared to Cliff.

Tessa placed the glasses on a tray and walked back to her station to distribute them.

She smiled at Edward. "May I take your order?"

"I'd like the club steak with smothered onions, a baked potato, and the peas in cream."

Tessa nodded. "That's a good selection." She moved on to the other customers. She was aware of Edward's eyes on her throughout the meal. Tessa kept busy as she served and conversed politely with each of her customers.

As Edward finished his meal, she approached. "Would you care for dessert?"

"I'll take a piece of apple pie. I don't suppose you have ice cream today?"

Tessa shook her head. "Not in this heat. We didn't have enough ice for the cooks to make ice cream today. We'll have ice delivered on Monday, but that doesn't help today. We do have whipped cream if you'd like that. "

"Yes, I'll have whipped cream."

Tessa nodded. She took the other orders then dished up the desserts.

As she set Edward's pie in front of him, she heard Cliff's deep voice in the foyer talking to Cora. "We've finished the threshing. It's been a long, hard two days."

Tessa tried to keep her attention on Edward but glanced up when Cliff stepped into the lunchroom doorway. He made eye contact with her and smiled his heart-stopping smile. Tessa's heart fluttered in her chest. What should she do? Edward was still there planning to spend the evening with her.

She stepped back to allow Edward to eat his pie. Drat that Harvey Girl contract--it stood firmly in the way of a relationship with either man! But it would help her tell Edward she couldn't court him.

As the other train passengers stood and left the lunchroom, Edward remained seated. He finished his pie, pushed back the plate, then took a drink of tea as Cliff made his way to her station. Anthony and Esther trailed behind him.

Edward leaned forward. "So, Tessa, can we visit after you get through here? I don't have to leave until tomorrow morning so I'll stay over in the employees' sleeping quarters in the freight depot."

Tessa looked directly at him and spoke politely, though she could see Cliff's frown out of the corner of her eye. "If you'll wait in the lobby, I'll join you when I'm finished."

Edward smiled as he pushed back his glass, gathered his jacket, and sauntered from the room.

Cliff scowled. "It's probably none of my business, but who was that? It was pretty forward of him to use your first name."

Tessa gathered the dirty dessert plates and glasses. "He's a friend I met in Topeka. He works for the railroad and is transferring to another station."

"Is this a special friend?"

"No, he's just a friend. As a Harvey Girl, I'm not supposed to have more than a friendship with gentlemen." Tessa turned and carried the dishes to the washroom. Indignation burned in her. How could Cliff McNance question her friends? He didn't have a claim on her. She grabbed the cleaning cloth from the soapy water and wrung it out with a vengeance.

Reason cleared her mind. He was a customer, and he had allowed her to spend time with his children. If she was honest with herself, she had to admit that she was attracted to him. She gave the cloth an extra twist. Why had fate brought both men here at the same time?

She hurried back to wipe the counter and reset it. Cliff,

Anthony, and Esther had seated themselves on the stools in her section.

"I'm sorry, Miss Gillespie. I was out of line. I have no right to question your friends." She glanced up at Cliff's brusque tone. His face was an unreadable mask.

"I appreciate your concern." Tessa smiled at him, then turned to Esther. "How are you? I've missed you all since you've been involved with the threshing."

"Hi, Miss Tessa. I'm fine. I helped Mrs. Unruh and Wanda serve the meals to the threshing crew. It was a lot of work, but it was fun to see that huge machine gobble up those stacks of wheat."

"That's what I heard. I'm proud of you. I know your daddy appreciated your help." Tessa looked toward the door. "Is Anna still sleeping? She fell asleep beside me in the deck chair earlier when we stopped for a water break."

Esther answered shyly. "No, she woke up. Grandma's feeding her and Charlie in Aunt Cora's office."

Tessa nodded then looked at Cliff. "How did the threshing go? I've been praying everything would run smoothly." Tessa laid menus in front of them.

"It was hard work, but no mishaps. We now have two granaries full of wheat and a wagon load parked in the barn ready to bring into town to sell. Anthony was an excellent helper. He drove the wagons."

"That's wonderful. At least the weather was good." Tessa moved to Anthony at the end of her section. "Hello, Anthony, I'll bet you're tired. What can I get you to drink?"

"Ah, I'm alright." He studied the menu. "I'll have some iced tea. I don't want any sugar."

Tessa adjusted his cup then moved on to her other customers.

She recognized Bill and Bertha Schuler and their two children from the church. She greeted them with a smile. "Hello, how are you this evening?"

Bertha spoke up. "We're doing okay. Just trying to stay cool. I didn't want to fire up the stove to fix supper, so we decided to eat at the Harvey House."

"A wonderful decision." Tessa turned to the children. "Your names are Will and Marie, right?"

They both nodded in agreement.

After they'd made their choices, Tessa returned to Cliff, Anthony, and Esther for their orders.

Cliff ordered a ham sandwich for himself and Esther, then turned to Mr. Schuler and was soon in deep conversation about the weather, wheat threshing, and city activities.

Tessa carried on her usual routine and served their meals. Esther yawned several times as she nibbled at her sandwich. Anthony consumed his pork loin sandwich and fried potatoes in record time then slumped back in his seat. They both looked like they could fall asleep in their chairs.

"You look exhausted. Threshing must be hard work."

Anthony glanced up at her and nodded. "We got up early to be ready for the threshers. They start at daybreak and work while it's cooler."

"And I had to get up to help Mrs. Unruh and Wanda. We cooked big meals for all those men." Esther gave another huge yawn.

Tessa smiled. "Do you want me to wrap up your sandwich so you can eat later?"

At her nod, Tessa hurried off to get some paper and a piece of string. When she returned, Cliff had finished his meal. Tessa turned toward him as she wrapped Esther's sandwich. "Would you like to finish with a piece of apple pie?"

He glanced at Anthony. "Sure. Bring a piece for me and

one for Anthony. He worked hard. I think Esther's too tired to eat."

Tessa watched Cliff as he and Anthony devoured the pie. She served dessert to the Schulers and gathered up the dirty plates. Even though his eyes showed tiredness and his hair had a sweat ring from his hat, he was the best-looking man she had ever seen. A shiver of trepidation shimmered through her. His words were sharper, his demeanor more formal since he'd seen her with Edward.

Cliff placed his napkin on his pie plate, finished his iced tea, then stood. "Come on you two. I need to get you home." He chuckled. "You look like you're about to fall off your stools."

He faced Tessa. "Thanks once again for serving us a great meal." He took a quarter from his pocket and placed it on the counter.

Esther gazed at Tessa. "Can I sit with you at church on Sunday?"

"Certainly, sweetheart, if it's alright with your daddy."

"Can I, Daddy?"

Cliff nodded curtly. "I suppose it's okay." He turned and walked toward the lunchroom door, followed by Anthony. Cliff lifted his hat from the hook by the door and placed it on his head. Esther slipped from her seat and hurried after them.

As they disappeared through the door, a knot of sadness settled in Tessa's stomach. Had she lost Cliff's friendship? *Was it just friendship?* If only Edward hadn't been here when Cliff arrived. She picked up the quarter and slipped it in her pocket then gathered the last of the dishes and carried them to the dish room.

When she had cleaned and straightened her area, she wiped her hands, smoothed her apron, and wandered into the lobby. Edward sat on a sofa near the middle of the room. He glanced up from the magazine in his hands as she approached and laid it on the small table beside him. He stood and motioned for her to sit in the chair across from him. "It's so good to see you, Tessa." He looked around the lobby. "This is a nice Harvey House. Is there a hotel upstairs?"

"Yes, it's called the Santa Fe Hotel. I do enjoy it here. The other Harvey Girls and the staff are great to work with. I like the city of Hutchinson as well." Tessa picked up one of the paper fans on the lamp table and waved it to keep cool. "So how have things been for you? Is this a promotion?"

Edward nodded as he sat back down. "I've been promoted to a machinist. I'll work in the large roundhouse in Las Vegas, New Mexico. It's my dream job--good money, adventure, and the opportunity to work on powerful locomotives."

"Congratulations. I'm happy for you."

Edward placed his arms on his knees and leaned forward. "Tessa, I need to tell you that I won't be able to continue our relationship. It just wouldn't be practical with the distance involved."

Tessa felt her shoulders relax in relief. "I completely under-stand. I've enjoyed our friendship, but I couldn't be more than a friend right now, anyway. I've signed a year contract as a Harvey Girl. There are strict rules about getting involved in romantic liaisons."

He sat back with a sigh. "I know that, but I was worried you'd be upset. I'm glad you understand. I hope we can continue as friends."

"I'd like that, too. One of the other Harvey Girls who trained with me was assigned to Las Vegas. Her name is Caro-line. Maybe you'll meet her."

"If I see her, I'll tell her hello from you." Edward smiled. "I hear it's a wild town; one of the largest in the region since the railroad built through there. It sounds exciting...maybe even a bit dangerous. I'll be in training, then I may be sent somewhere else along the line."

Tessa nodded. "I wish you all the luck in the world. Thanks for stopping on your way. It was fun to visit with you again."

"Well, I guess I better go." Edward stood and reached for Tessa's hand to assist her up beside him. "I'll be in for an early breakfast before the train leaves."

"Good. I'll get the opportunity to say goodbye." Tessa walked with him to the door.

She turned, slowly, and ambled across the lobby. Her stomach knotted and the back of her throat ached with dread at the thought of Cliff's guarded expression and abrupt manner. Had she lost his friendship? *Was it more than friendship or would someone else grab his attention?* She enjoyed the banter with him when he came into the lunchroom, and she already loved his precious children.

Tessa frowned. What else could she have done? Edward had been a perfect gentleman. It would've been rude to refuse to see him.

CHAPTER 6

Cliff frowned as he stepped into the lobby from the lunch-room. The well-dressed man Tessa had declared was her friend sat on one of the sofas reading a magazine.

Cliff shook his head. He was a fool to think he'd have a chance with Tessa. She was beautiful and probably had any number of men waiting to court her. Besides, she'd signed that Harvey Girl contract.

He strode to the registration desk where Cora stood with Charlie in her arms. She smiled. "Are you ready to go?"

"Yes, I have to get Anthony and Esther home before they fall asleep standing up. They've had two very long days. I'm relieved the threshing's done."

"I'll bet you are. It's good to have the wheat put up." Cora handed Charlie to Cliff. "Anna's with her grandma in my office. I'll go get her. The kids both ate supper."

Cliff chuckled. "Your mother's probably ready for a break, too. Charlie and Anna can be a handful."

A few minutes later, Cora returned with Mrs. Dickenson and Anna.

Cliff nodded to his mother-in-law. "How are you doing,

ma'am? Did these rascals wear you completely out? I appreciate your caring for them while I had the threshers there. It was crazy."

"They were well-behaved. I enjoyed having them. The farm was no place for them with wagons coming and going." She handed him a small bag. "Here are their clothes."

Cliff nodded, then led the children across the lobby to the door. He glanced toward the lunchroom. He wanted to be gone before Tessa appeared to visit with her gentleman friend.

The sun was sinking in the western sky as he herded his brood across the porch and to the carriage. He loved each one of them dearly, but they were a big responsibility. How could he expect a young woman to come in and take on their care, cooking, and cleaning? He'd briefly considered placing an ad in one of the big eastern papers for a mail-order bride. But the thought of marrying a woman he didn't even know horrified him. He'd rather stay single and carry on by himself.

Esther, Anna, and Charlie clambered up onto the back seat of the carriage and Anthony swung up beside his father.

Cliff looked at his son. "Do you want to drive? Maybe that will help you stay awake."

"I'd love to drive. I'm awake now. I've been practicing with the wagons." Anthony took the reins that his father relinquished.

"You were a great help these last couple of days. I'm proud of you."

Anthony pulled on the reins and backed Babe away from the hitching post, then guided her out of the lot and onto the street. They headed out of town.

Cliff surveyed the brown pastures. They were in critical need of rain. If this heat continued there wouldn't be enough grass to keep the livestock fed. He didn't want to start using the winter reserves this soon. He'd been praying for rain, but it was about as hard to come by as a wife. God didn't seem to be answering his requests these days.

"Pa?"

Anthony's voice drew Cliff from his thoughts. "Yes, son, what is it?"

"Why did Ma have to die? Sometimes I just miss her so much it hurts. I love Charlie and all, but I wish Ma hadn't died when he was born."

"I've asked that same question many times. I wish I had the answer. The only thing I can say is that God knows what He's doing. He had to have a reason."

"Do you ever feel mad at God for taking her away?"

"I did a lot, at first. But I know your ma's happy in Heaven. She loved Jesus so much, and now she's with Him. As much as I miss her, I wouldn't ask her to come back. That's why it's so important that we believe Jesus died on the cross for our sins. We can go to Heaven and see her when we die. We have to ask Him to forgive our sins and be our Savior."

"I'm not sure I've ever done that."

"Oh, son, that's the most important thing you could ever do. When we get home, I'll get my Bible and show you how you can be saved."

Anthony nodded. "Do you think we'll ever get a new ma? I don't think I could love another one, not like I loved Ma."

Cliff shifted on the seat so he could look at Anthony. "I'd like to get married again. I was happy with your ma. It's been lonely without her. It's not easy raising four young kids all by myself. But a woman would have to love all of you, and me, and God, before I'd consider it." He placed his hand on Anthony's knee. "I figured it'd be hard for you to call her 'Ma', and that's okay."

"Billy's pa put an ad in the paper. His ma came from Pennsylvania."

"I don't want to do that." Cliff turned back toward the front of the carriage. "I'd want to know her well before I married her. God hasn't shown me the right one, yet." At least he didn't think so. He'd hoped Tessa might be the one. She was beautiful inside and out, and she'd connected with his children. However, that hadn't worked out. If only he'd met her before she signed that contract.

He'd prayed about the other eligible women in the church. There was no way he wanted to marry any of them. His neighbor had a spinster daughter who constantly tried to push herself on him. She'd offered her help more than once, but he hadn't felt anything special for her and steered clear whenever possible.

As Anthony turned into the drive, Cliff surveyed the clapboard house that he'd built before his marriage to Ella. He and his brother, Paul, had moved from their family's home in Ohio when they heard about available land in Kansas. Cliff had decided to stay near the community of Hutchinson. His brother decided to move farther south and start a ranch.

On his first Sunday in Hutchinson, Cliff had met Ella at the church where she attended with her family. He'd known immediately that he wanted the vivacious young lady to be his wife. This fertile section of land, with a creek running through it, had been a fortunate find. He'd built the house and barn with the help of his new neighbors. A year later, he and Ella were married and moved into the new home.

He grimaced. When Ella was alive, there were always flowers growing along the walkway. Now there was just dry grass, weeds, and dirt.

Anthony stopped the horse and carriage in front of the house. He, expectantly, turned to his pa. "How'd I do?"

"You did a great job." Cliff climbed down. "I'll take the younguns in the house. You take Babe to the barn. I'll be out to help milk as soon as I get them settled." He turned toward the back seat and smiled. Esther was sound asleep, her head against the side of the carriage, with Charlie snuggled up next to her snoring softly.

Anna scrambled off the seat and into his arms. "They went to sleep, but I didn't. I'm not sleepy."

"You already had your nap, you little scamp." Cliff set her down. "If you are so wide awake, you can walk on into the house while I get your brother and sister." He picked up Charlie then gently shook Esther. "Wake up, sleepyhead. Why don't you go on in and get into your pajamas? It's going to be dark soon."

Esther climbed down and trudged into the house while Cliff followed with Charlie and Anna. "You all need to get ready for bed."

A short while later, he left the house with the milk bucket. He hated to leave the little ones alone since Esther was already asleep, but there was nothing else to do. The cows had to be milked. He and Anthony would get back in as soon as possible.

When he reached the barn, Bossy was in her stall, but Bessy and Anthony were missing. Anthony must've had to find her and bring her in. Cliff began milking. He finished and waited by the doorway, as Bessy ambled in. Anthony was on her heels; a scowl on his face. "Dumb cow! She was clear at the other end of the pasture. I should have just left her there."

Cliff smiled. "I'm glad you didn't." He guided the wayward cow into her stall and milked her. His mind was on Charlie and Anna in the house. Hopefully, they weren't getting into mischief.

He glanced at his pocket watch as they walked toward the house. It had been a full forty-five minutes. Much longer than he'd planned. He set the full milk bucket on the table and headed toward the children's bedroom. As he walked into the room, cold fear clutched his heart. Esther and Charlie were sound asleep, but Anna was gone.

He rushed back out into the parlor. The lantern was lit on the table beside the sofa. "Anna, where are you?" He strode into the kitchen and looked in every corner, under the table, and in the pantry. "Anna, this isn't funny. Where did you go?"

Anthony grabbed the lantern and hurried to check their bedrooms. "She's not here. Do you want me to check outside?"

"Yes, look around the house and maybe out toward the barn. I'll look in their room again."

As he walked in, he heard a giggle. He stopped and listened. Another giggle, then a little voice. "I'm under here."

Cliff caught his breath and felt as if his knees might give away. "Anna Louise, you get out here right now! You nearly scared the life out of me. Don't you ever do that again!" He watched as she scooted out from under the bed, not sure whether to spank or hug her. He snatched her up and gave her a shake, then pulled her to him in a hug. "If you ever do that again, you *will* get spanked. I thought you were lost."

"I was playing hide-and-seek."

"Well, it wasn't a good game. Don't play it again, especially when you're supposed to be in bed. Now we have to find your brother. He's outside looking for you."

Twenty minutes later, Cliff collapsed, with a sigh, on his sofa. He was exhausted but unable to sleep. He'd already been worn out from threshing, and then Anna had nearly scared him to death with her little stunt.

Anthony, too, was dead tired after he rounded up Bessy. He'd nearly fallen into bed and Cliff had to remind him to put on his pajamas. There'd been no time to share the Bible verses about salvation. He bowed his head. *Father God, I need Your guidance and help. You have given me these precious children to care for and protect, but I can't do it on my own. Please, please show me the woman who should be my wife. I know in Your infinite wisdom, You know who she is.* He sat quietly, his elbows propped on his knees and his face in his hands. A vision of Tessa, as he'd seen her that first day, gazing at his little Esther, appeared in his mind. *God, I thought Tessa was the one. I think I'm beginning to love her. She's so beautiful and kind. But she has a contract, and even maybe other men in her life. Why do things have to be so complicated?* His shoulders slumped in despair.

"Pa?"

Cliff sat up and studied Anthony as he walked from his room. "I thought you'd be asleep by now."

Anthony frowned. "I couldn't sleep. You told me you'd show me those verses about how to be saved. I want to be able to see Ma in Heaven someday."

Cliff patted the seat beside him then picked up his Bible from the lamp table. "Sit down." He faced Anthony, opened the Bible, and flipped through the pages. "I know you want to see your ma, but that can't be the reason you ask Jesus to be your Savior. You have to know that you're a sinner. Here, read Romans 3:23. He pointed at the words.

Anthony read slowly, "*For all have sinned, and come short of the glory of God.*"

"The Bible says that we have all sinned. Do you know you have done things that don't please God, like lying or taking something that didn't belong to you?"

Anthony nodded. "Yes, I've told lies, and I took Billy's beanie flipper. He left it lying on the ball field at school, and I picked it up. It was a lot nicer than mine. When he went to look for it, I didn't tell him I had it." Anthony looked down, a miserable expression on his face.

"Do you think that was a sin?"

Anthony nodded again.

"Do you think God was pleased with that?"

"No, but now I don't know what to do about it."

"Do you know that God knew you were going to take that beanie flipper long before you were born? In Romans 5:8 it says, *But God commendeth--that means* showed--*his love toward us, in that, while we were yet sinners, Christ died for us.* Did you know Jesus died on the cross for you even though he knew you would be a sinner?"

Anthony shook his head. "No. Why did He do that?"

"Do you know the verse, John 3:16?"

"Yes. *For God so loved the world, that He gave His only begotten Son, that whosoever believeth in him should not perish, but have everlasting life.*"

"He did it because He loved you so much he wanted you to be able to go to Heaven and live forever, the same as Ma. But you have to believe that He died for your sins. You have to ask Him to forgive your sins and be your Savior. He'll come inside you and help you do what's right. Do you want to pray now?"

Anthony nodded. "Yeah, I do." He bowed his head. "God, I know I sinned and I believe that Jesus knew about my sin and died on the cross because He loved me. Please forgive me and come inside me to help me do better. Amen." He looked up with relief shining on his face. "I'll take Billy's beany flipper back to him on Sunday. I hope he won't be mad. I'll tell him about Jesus."

Cliff hugged him. "I'm proud and happy for you, son. You won't have to worry about not going to Heaven to see Ma. But now you better get back to bed. You won't want to get up in the morning."

TESSA SCANNED the parking lot as she walked up to the church with the other girls on Sunday. Would Cliff even talk to her? She cringed. Why did Edward have to be there when Cliff came in on Friday evening? Thank goodness, Edward only wanted to be friends. She had a clear conscience about their friendship and how they had parted.

At that moment, Cliff walked around the corner of the church with Charlie in his arms. Tessa sucked in her breath and her heart skipped a beat. *He was the perfect picture of manhood and fatherhood.* Sadness flooded her as he briefly caught her gaze then looked away. She bit her lip.

Esther ran toward her and wrapped her in a bear hug. "Hi, Miss Tessa. Pa said I can sit with you." She glanced back over her shoulder at her father. "If I'm good."

"Alright. We better find a seat." Tessa glanced at Cliff as she followed the other Harvey Girls to the church door. Cora had taken Anna's hand and Cliff walked behind her. Tessa arrived at the entrance at the same time he did.

Cliff reached to hold the door. "Hello, Miss Gillespie. How are you this fine morning?"

"I'm fine." She wanted to scream, *Don't be so formal!* As she ushered Esther through the doorway, two young boys barreled up the steps and jostled their way into the church. Tessa was pushed sideways against Cliff's arm. At the contact with his firm muscle, an acute awareness flooded through her and sent a tingling shock wave to her fingers.

Cliff took her arm to steady her.

Tessa felt her eyes widen as she looked at him. "Thank you. I'm sorry. Those boys…"

He smiled. "I noticed. Think nothing of it. They were just thoughtless." He guided her into the church and walked with her and Esther to the Harvey Girl pew then slid into the pew behind them.

Tessa stared straight ahead at the stained glass window behind the baptistry. Her arm still tingled from his touch.

What was this sensation? She focused on the Good Shepherd that was pictured in the window. *Jesus, what do I do? I've committed to being a Harvey Girl, and yet I feel this connection with Cliff and his children. I, at least, want to be his friend. Please guide me.*

Esther pushed her hand up under Tessa's arm. "I'm glad you're my friend."

Tessa put her other hand over Esther's fingers. "I'm glad I have you for a friend, too." She smiled to herself. Cliff couldn't ignore her completely if his children wanted to be around her.

The pastor's message was taken from 1 John 3:17-18: "*But whoso hath this world's good, and seeth his brother have need, and shutteth up his bowels of compassion from him, how dwelleth the love of God in him. My little children, let us not love in word, neither in tongue; but in deed and in truth.:*

Tessa bowed her head. "*Lord, I don't understand these feelings in my heart, but I want to have Your love dwelling in me. Show me what you want me to do.*"

Wednesday, after the morning rush, Cora walked into the dining room with a handful of envelopes. "Girls, I have your pay for the month." She grinned at Tessa. "This is your first payday, isn't it? Are you excited?"

Tessa set down the cups and saucers she was gathering and took the coveted envelope. "Yes. I've been waiting for this. I want to send some of it home for my family."

"I figured you might. Several of the girls will walk to the post office this afternoon if you'd like to get it mailed. I have envelopes and stamps at my desk."

"That sounds like a wonderful idea." Tessa slipped the money into her pocket and picked up the tray containing the dirty dishes. "When I get this cleaned up I'll write my parents a letter."

Cora ambled around the room and distributed the pay envelopes to the other girls then returned to Tessa's table. Tessa set clean tablecloths on a chair and gathered up the soiled ones.

Cora squinted her eyes as if in thought, then spoke. "Tessa, so this Edward that came the other evening. Is he special to you?"

Tessa stopped and faced her. She shook her head. "No. He accompanied me to a couple of Harvey Girl activities while I was in Topeka, but he's been transferred to New Mexico. We won't stay in communication. It's too far away. I'm not disappointed. I didn't care for him in a romantic sense."

Cora nodded and relaxed her shoulders. She picked up the clean tablecloth and helped Tessa spread it on the table. "Cliff had quite a scare the other evening after he'd been here to pick up the children. Esther was so tired she went directly to bed. Cliff put Anna and Charlie in bed and went out to milk. When he and Anthony returned to the house, he couldn't find Anna. She'd had her nap, and she wasn't tired."

Tessa sucked in her breath. "Was she okay? Where was she? She was at church Sunday."

"Cliff and Anthony searched the house, and Anthony even went outside to check around. Then Cliff found the little stinker hiding under her bed." Cora chuckled. "She thought it was a game. She was playing hide-and-seek."

"Oh, my goodness! I'll bet her father didn't think it was a game."

"No, he didn't! That man needs a wife to help with those children. I told him he should marry Philomena Bartel from the church. She's about his age, but he won't hear of it. Something's going to happen to one of those younguns out there all by themselves."

Tessa shuddered at the thought of one of them injured, or worse, killed. She gave a weak nod.

Cora gathered up the dirty linen. "Here, I'll take these to the laundry chute for you. I've kept you from your work, and you want to get that letter written."

Tessa stood and watched Cora as she strolled across the dining room. *Why had Cora told her that? What if something happened to one of those precious children?* She couldn't bear the thought. *She also couldn't bear the thought of Cliff getting married to some other woman.* She nearly stopped breathing, and her mouth dropped open at the thought. Did she...could she...be falling in love with this man she had only known for a month? *Was it possible?* Did he love her? She quickly gathered the items for her tables and set them for dinner, then hurried up to her room. She took out a sheet of paper and a pencil, items she'd bought at the mercantile with her tip money, and carried them to the small desk in the parlor.

She sat and stared at the blank page. What could she write? She couldn't tell them she was thinking of giving up her job as a Harvey Girl to get married. They wouldn't understand that. She didn't understand it, either.

If she gave up her job she wouldn't have any money for her family, and she wouldn't be able to go home and see them after she'd worked six months. It was all totally crazy. She didn't even know if Cliff wanted to marry her. He didn't want to marry that woman in the church, she smiled at that thought.

After a few minutes, she put the burning question and her churning emotions from her mind and began to write.

July 29, 1885

Dear Pa, Ma, Margaret, Abigail, Theresa, Lucile, Betsy, and Samuel,

How are you all doing? I hope you are well. I miss you and enjoyed your letter on my birthday.

I have been very busy, but I like it here in Hutchinson. I've made a lot of good friends. I received my first payment today and I wanted to send some money to you.

Give my sisters and brother hugs for me. There is a family here who has children about the ages of Theresa, Lucile, Betsy, and Samuel. It makes me miss you all.

I love you,

Tessa

She folded the letter and slipped the ten-dollar bill in it then walked back down to the registration desk where Cora sat writing in a ledger.

She waited until Cora looked up. "May I please have an envelope and stamp? When will the girls go to the post office?"

Cora retrieved the items from her desk. "They'll go after dinner. Hannah knows you want to go. She'll tell you."

Tessa nodded as she slipped the letter into the envelope. She wrote the address on the front with the pencil and attached the stamp.

CHAPTER 7

Cliff dipped up five bowls of oatmeal and set them on the table with a pitcher of milk. Then he picked up Charlie and sat him on his chair. "Anthony, Esther, Anna come and eat. The day's getting away."

Anna peeked around the doorsill. "Can I bring my baby?"

"No, lay it on the sofa. You can play with her after breakfast."

Anthony wandered in and sat down. "Esther's still in bed."

"Go get her. I need to take that load of wheat into town. I've put it off too long already."

"Can I go with you?" Anthony watched his pa.

"No, you stay here and help with the younguns. You can help keep an eye on them. After breakfast, I want you to saddle Babe and ride over to get Wanda. I told her Ma that I'd need her today."

Anthony frowned. "Aww. Alright. Can I walk Sassy in the horse pasture when I get back?"

"Yes, just stay within earshot." Cliff went to the parlor door. "Esther, come and eat."

Esther walked in, sleepy-eyed, her hair in a tangled disarray.

She curled her lip. "Why do we have to have oatmeal again? I don't like oatmeal. I want eggs."

"Oatmeal's what we have and that's what you'll eat. Anthony's going to go get Wanda to stay with you today. I have errands to run in town."

Esther scowled. "I'm not hungry."

"I guess you'll just go without, then."

A half-hour later, Cliff hitched Dobbin, his workhorse, to the wagon. He'd been busy this last week cultivating the east field and hadn't had time to haul the wheat into town. The morning heat was already building and a warm breeze blew from the south.

Anthony rode Babe up the drive with Wanda perched behind him. She slid off the horse in front of the house. Esther, Anna, and Charlie ran out to meet her as Anthony trotted Babe on out to the barn. Wanda took Charlie's hand and the children all headed toward the chicken coop.

Cliff took the horse's reins as Anthony dismounted. "Here, I'll take care of Babe before I leave. Thank you for going to get Wanda." He patted Anthony on the back. "Go have fun with Sassy."

He smiled as Anthony took off on a dead run. Cliff watched Anthony, in the paddock, as he unsaddled Babe and led her to her stall. The boy was leading the young filly around in circles with a halter rope. He'd told Anthony he could have her if he'd spend time and train her. They were going to make a fine team.

Merry laughter rang out from the direction of the chicken coop. Wanda and the children must be out there. Gertrude, one of the chickens that had hatched in the spring, was tame. She'd run to the children when they entered the pen. Esther especially loved that chicken. She picked it up and carried it around at every opportunity. Cliff shook his head. He'd never seen anything like it.

As he drove toward the house, Wanda and the younger children ran to meet him. He stopped and leaned over the side. "You all be careful and stay out of trouble. I'll be back this afternoon. There's stew in the pot on the back of the stove for dinner."

Wanda nodded. "We'll be fine."

Cliff drove out of the yard and headed toward Hutchinson. He needed to sell the wheat and get some supplies, but the main reason for his haste was to find Tessa. Cora had informed him of her conversation with Tessa about her friend, Edward. Cliff smiled. Edward wasn't an obstacle after all. He felt light with relief.

The problem of the Harvey House contract remained. And he wasn't confident about Tessa's feelings for him. He'd seen her exhibit love for his children but he wanted her to love him. A marriage of convenience did not appeal to him. He wanted a life built on mutual love.

Twenty minutes later, he pulled into town and drove down Main Street toward the grain elevator on the south end of town. When he arrived, another load waited ahead of him. Cliff climbed down and walked to the other wagon. The driver was a neighbor who had helped on the threshing crew. "Howdy, neighbor. Howard Schmidt, isn't it? If I help you shovel your load, will you give me a hand?"

"Sounds like a plan. I'll be pleased to help." Howard drove his wagon over the large scale so the attendant could weigh his load then on up to the waiting rail car. The three of them shoveled and made short work of the transfer. Thirty minutes later, both wagons sat empty and weighed, and Cliff had received his money. It was eleven-thirty according to his pocket watch. After he purchased his groceries and supplies at the mercantile, it would be dinner time at the Harvey House. He was beyond ready.

Only one space remained at the hitching rail when he pulled into the parking lot an hour later. Train passengers streamed from the Santa Fe Hotel and back to the waiting train. He secured Babe, picked up his dinner jacket, and made his way into the lobby.

Cora was busy collecting money from departing patrons while the manager directed the local customers. Cliff stood to one side. As the last of the train people left, Cora turned to him. "I suppose you want to sit at Tessa's table. She's in the dining room today."

Cliff smiled at her. "Thanks, Cora. I may have to steal one of your Harvey Girls." He slipped on his jacket and placed his hat on the rack. "That is if she'll have me."

"Cliff McNance, you watch yourself. She may not want to give up all her working girl advantages."

"I know. That's the problem." He grimaced as he turned toward the dining-room door.

Cora directed a couple to a table so Cliff walked in behind them. He scanned the room until he located Tessa toward the back. Her face was animated as she visited with the four people already at her table. Cliff hesitated, mesmerized by her grace and charm.

She looked up as he made his way across the room and a beautiful smile illuminated her face. "Cliff, what are you doing here in the middle of the week?" She looked behind him. "Did you bring any of the children?"

Cliff grinned. "No, I came to see you."

Tessa chuckled. "I know better than to think you came all the way into town just to see me."

"Actually, I brought a load of wheat into the grain elevator to sell. Anthony and Wanda are with the children at home." He sat at the table. "I hoped to see you before I returned to the farm. I'm sorry I've been such a grouch."

"It's okay. I'm glad to see you smile, though. You want iced tea, right? " At his nod, Tessa adjusted his cup then turned to welcome more guests. Soon her tables were filled and she took food orders from them.

As Cliff loitered over his beef stroganoff and noodles, his mind was spinning. He needed to know if Tessa would even consider giving up her job to be his wife.

As she set a piece of cherry pie in front of him, he touched her hand. "Tessa, I want to talk to you. Not today, because I have to get back home, but soon."

Tessa straightened. "You want to talk to me?" She hesitated. "Maybe we could talk Sunday afternoon."

Cliff nodded. "That should work. I'll let you know on Sunday morning."

A commotion outside the door of the dining room drew their attention. "Aunt Cora, is Pa here? I saw his wagon outside." Anthony's frightened voice rang, clearly, throughout the room. "I need him!"

Fear rumbled through Cliff as he pushed his chair back. He stood, strode across the dining room, and burst through the door into the lobby.

Cora met him at the door with her arm around Anthony.

Anthony ran to his father. "Pa, Esther tried to help Wanda with the stew and she spilled it down her leg and foot. Wanda cleaned it, but, Pa, Esther's leg is burned bad! It's got a big ole blister! We didn't know what to do so we got her in the carriage and came to you." He let out a sob. "She's cryin' and cryin'."

"You did the right thing, son. Let's get her to the doctor."

Just then Tessa rushed through the door. "What happened?" Fear etched her face.

Cora stopped her. "I'll tell you, but first, I need to get Anna and Charlie." She turned. "Cliff, you and Anthony get Esther to the doctor."

When they reached the carriage, Cliff examined Esther's leg. It had an angry red wound covered with a massive blister from above the knee to the top of her foot. She was whimpering in pain. Wanda sat beside her on the back seat. Cora helped Anna and Charlie down while Cliff grabbed the reins, and he and Anthony climbed up on the front seat.

"We'll get you to Doctor Snyder, sweetheart. He's just up the street." He pulled out of the lot, trotted the horse up the two blocks to the doctor's building, and quickly carried her up the stairs to his office.

The doctor directed them into his examining room and Cliff set her on the table.

"Well, young lady, what did you do? That's a nasty burn."

Wanda stepped forward. "She spilled a bowl of hot soup down her leg. I should have carried it for her, but she had it before I could stop her."

"It's not your fault, Wanda." Cliff waved her and Anthony into the waiting room. "You two wait here." He shut the door.

Doctor Snyder got a basin of cool water and a soft cloth. "I need to clean the burned area. The cool water will soothe the pain a bit. The most important thing is to be careful of the blister. She won't be as apt to get a fever or infection if we keep that intact. Can she stay in town somewhere?"

"Yes, her grandmother lives here. She can stay with her."

"I just learned about a new medication. It's called Carron oil; a mixture of lime-water liniment mixed with linseed oil. There've been good results with it. We'll soak strips of cotton and place them over the burn. They'll have to be changed daily. Cool water around the edges can help with the pain. I'll also give her laudanum to help with pain and to keep her from thrashing about."

TESSA SHUDDERED at the expression of fear and anguish on Anthony's face. She felt compelled to go to Esther but knew she was on duty.

Cora walked back into the lobby with Charlie and Anna. "They're on their way to the doctor." She waved toward the dining room. "Go finish your tables. I'll let you know what's happening as soon as I know something. We can't do anything right now but pray."

"I'll certainly do that." Tessa took deep breaths to steady her nerves as she walked slowly across the dining room to her area. The patrons watched as she approached. "I'm sorry, folks. I shouldn't have left so suddenly, but my friend's little girl got seriously burned. She's very special to me." She smiled. "Can I get anything else for you? Here, let me refill your drinks."

As the local customers stood, several of them spoke words of concern and support before they strolled toward the dining-room door. Tessa took a shaky breath and felt tears gather in her eyes. Not sure her knees would hold her up, she sat in the nearest chair. *Lord, please don't let Esther get a fever. She's such a precious little girl, and I love her so much. Lord God, if it could be your will, I want to be her Mama.* She stopped and let the tears flow. *I do love Cliff! I know now. I want to marry him and be a mother to his children!*

She pulled out her handkerchief and wiped her eyes as Hannah stepped up beside her. "What happened?"

"Cliff's little girl, Esther, spilled a hot bowl of soup down her leg. She's got an ugly burn."

Hannah grimaced. "Oooh! That sounds horrible! I hate burns."

"Me, too. She's at the doctor's right now." Tessa stood and cleared the dishes from her tables. She needed to reset them, then she'd go help Cora with Charlie and Anna. She had to do something to keep her mind occupied.

When she had everything in place for the next meal, she hurried toward Cora's office. Anna was sitting at the desk drawing a picture and Charlie had crawled under the desk. He was making meowing sounds like a kitten. Tessa chuckled. "Are you a kitty?"

Charlie nodded then crawled out and pawed her leg.

Tessa turned to Cora. "Would it be okay if I take Charlie out onto the porch and let him play? He'll have more room to run off his energy."

Cora nodded. "That'd be wonderful." She handed Tessa a wooden train engine. "Here, he can play with this. One of the signalmen carved it and gave it to me."

Tessa sat on one of the deck chairs as Charlie galloped up and down the porch whinnying like a horse. Love flowed through her. *God, is it possible that I could be a mother to these little ones? I'd surely count it a privilege.*

When Hannah and Sarah slipped out to sit with her, Charlie wandered over and pushed the toy locomotive along the deck boards with a chugging sound.

Hannah leaned over and watched him. "He's so cute. Cliff has adorable children. It's too bad he hasn't remarried. They need a mother."

Tessa gazed at him and nodded. "Yes, they do."

"They're crazy about you, Tessa." Sarah studied her. "I think Cliff loves you! He can't keep his eyes off of you when he comes into the dining room. We've noticed it for a while." She winked at Hannah, who nodded in agreement.

Tessa sat forward. "Do you think so? I just don't know. I'd love to marry him and be a mother to these precious little ones." She hesitated. "I don't know how Anthony would react. I haven't spent much time with him. He might find it harder to accept me since he's older." She grimaced. "And then there's my contract."

"What do you think God wants you to do?" Hannah gazed at her.

"I don't know. I've been praying about it."

"Then God will show you."

Tessa nodded as Charlie crawled up into her lap and yawned.

Sarah grinned. "I think you may have your answer."

The three of them visited as Charlie slept on Tessa's shoulder.

A little while later, Cora and Anna stepped out onto the porch. "How's it going out here? We needed a little fresh air. It's hard to wait for news." She looked at Charlie on Tessa's lap. "You have the touch with these little tykes."

"They're so cuddly. I used to do this with my brother and sister."

Hannah pointed. "Here comes Cliff."

Within minutes, Cliff and Wanda walked up the steps. Tessa leaned forward. "How's Esther?"

Cliff heaved a sigh and his shoulders slumped. "She's okay right now. The doctor put some new medicine on the burn and gave her laudanum to help her sleep. He said it's a miracle the blister didn't break while getting her into the carriage and all. If we can keep the blister from bursting she won't be as apt to get the fever." He turned to Wanda. "These young folks were very responsible. I'm proud of them."

Tessa shifted Charlie's position. "Where's Esther now?"

"She's at Grandma Dickenson's house. Anthony stayed to help her." He turned to Cora. "Will it be alright if I leave Anna and Charlie here for a while? I have to take Wanda home, milk the cows, and get some clothes for us. I'm going to stay in town. Grandma Dickenson said we could stay there."

Cora nodded. "Mr. McKinsey said we can keep Anna and Charlie here at the Harvey House. They don't need to be underfoot at Mom's while Esther requires rest and quiet. I'll make a pallet on the floor of my room. They'll have lots of babysitters here."

"Are you sure it's okay?"

"Yes, if there's a question, Mr. McKinsey will explain it to Mr. Harvey."

CHAPTER 8

Tessa hurried into Cora's office. She had finished with the Saturday noon rush and set her tables for the next train stop. Cora sat at her desk and wrote in a ledger, while Anna and Charlie napped on her bed.

Tessa smiled at the children as she settled back in the chair beside Cora's desk. They had so much attention at the Harvey House and played hard. They needed a nap. She turned to Cora. "Have you heard anything from Cliff? Is there any change with Esther?"

Cora stuck her pen in the inkwell and sat back. "Cliff and Anthony ate in the lunchroom. Cliff wanted to talk to you, but you were busy and they didn't have time to stay. He said he'd see you later."

"I'm sorry I missed him. Did he say how Esther is doing?"

"She's doing as well as possible. The blister got a small tear and was seeping fluid, but the doctor put some medicine on it to stop the leak. He wasn't too concerned about it as long as they could keep it from tearing any farther. She sat up in a chair today, but the doctor doesn't want her to walk. He'll allow her to sit in a tub of cool water before he changes her dressings.

It helps with the pain and soaks the dressings so they don't pull the blister away."

Tessa cringed and pursed her lips. "That sounds horrible. I pray she doesn't get a fever. I wish I could do something more to help. Maybe I can stay with her tomorrow during church so their family can attend. I wonder how long it will take the burn to heal?"

"The doctor said the blister should start going down in about a week." Cora studied her. "It's obvious this is affecting you deeper than the average person. Why is that?"

Tessa sighed, hesitated, then spoke. "In the short time I've been here, I've learned to love those children. I had an instant connection with Esther. She reminds me of myself at that age. I took on so many responsibilities when my mother was injured. It's not an easy age." Tessa watched as Charlie took a deep shuddery breath in his sleep. "And the little ones are so easy to love."

"They need a mother." Cora cocked her head and watched Tessa. "And Cliff needs a wife and helper."

Warmth crept up into Tessa's face. She didn't answer. What could she say? She wanted to be their mother, but she'd signed that contract.

"I think Cliff would like for you to be that wife and mother." Cora stood, moved from behind her desk, and hugged Tessa. "I may be speaking out of turn, but I can't help but ask...how do you feel about that?"

Tessa glanced at Cora, then back toward the sleeping children. "I'd be thrilled at the idea, but how can I? I signed that contract and I feel an obligation to keep my word."

"Do you love Cliff? He's said more than once that he would only marry for love."

Tessa ducked her head and stared at her clasped hands in her lap. "I don't know him well, but I think I do. I look forward to the times I can be around him and hear him talk, but how do you know? I had never been around men until Edward. He was a friend and co-worker, but my feelings were never what they are for Cliff. I didn't want to spend my life with Edward, but I think I do want that with Cliff."

Cora gave Tessa a final squeeze. "If you decide you love him and want to marry him, I think Fred Harvey would let you break your contract. He's aware of the situation."

Tessa sat up and stared at her. "Really, do you think so?" Then she chuckled. "That may be getting the cart before the horse. He hasn't asked me to marry him. Maybe he doesn't want me."

Cora grinned impishly. "I don't believe for a minute that's a problem." She returned to her desk. "Would you watch Anna and Charlie for an hour or so this evening? I need to go home for a bit. I'll mention about you staying with Esther while we go to church in the morning."

SUNDAY MORNING, Tessa sat on the porch and waited for Cliff to pick her up. It was early--a perfect opportunity to enjoy the sunrise and some quiet time with her thoughts.

Grandma Dickenson and Cliff had agreed that she could stay with Esther while they went to church. He would take her to the Dickenson home, then return for Cora and the children.

She smiled and stood as he drove into the parking lot. A warm glow enveloped her at the sight of him. She loved spending time with him. She walked down the steps as he approached then hurried down the walkway. "Hi, Cliff. How's Esther this morning?" She fell into step with him as he took her arm to guide her toward the carriage.

"She's feeling much better. She slept well last night without any pain medicine, and she wanted to sit up in the chair this morning. She's excited that you're coming to stay with her. You're one of her favorite people." He gave her arm a gentle squeeze. "I'm glad you'll be there. I agree with her. You are special."

"Your children are just easy to love. I'm nothing special. " She chuckled as he assisted her into the carriage. "Charlie and Anna quickly became favorites of the Harvey House staff. They never lack attention. Sam and Henry, our head cook and baker, have delighted in making treats for them. Last night they each had a sugar cookie."

Cliff shook his head and sighed. "I'll never get them under control after all that attention." He walked around the carriage and climbed into the driver's seat.

"I don't know. I think they'll be ready to get back with their family."

Cliff pulled out of the parking lot and drove up Main Street. He reached over and took Tessa's hand. "Would you consider…? Is there a chance… Oh, I wasn't going to say anything this morning."

"What, Cliff?"

He shook his head. "I wondered if you'd want to be a part of that family? I know it's asking a lot. Don't answer now. If it's alright, we can talk about it this afternoon after dinner. There's no time now."

"It's fine. I want to talk to you." Tessa gave his hand a slight squeeze while her insides fluttered. "But, right now, we better get to Esther, and you need to get to church."

Cliff turned onto First Street and drove beside the trolley tracks.

Tessa took in the grand houses that lined the streets. There were two-and-three-storied homes with wide expansive porches, delightful landscaping, and elaborate carriage houses. "These are beautiful homes."

"Yes, they are. William and Mildred Dickenson were among the first settlers in Hutchinson even before the city was founded. Mr. Dickenson was a friend of C.C. Hutchinson, the city's founder. They lived here when I arrived in 1870. They've since built a much larger home." Cliff pulled the carriage into the drive beside a two-storied white frame house.

Tessa could hardly believe her eyes. An elegant covered porch and bay window adorned the front of the house and she glimpsed a screened-in sunroom extending along the side and back. Bushes and flowers along the foundation gave a warm invitation to family and friends.

Cliff slid from his seat, tied the horse to the hitching post then assisted Tessa. They walked to the door which led to the sunroom. He opened it and motioned her to enter. The room was decorated with plants and comfortable chairs. Sunlight flooded in the windows and a light breeze wafted through. Esther sat in an overstuffed chair with her leg elevated on a hassock.

Tessa hurried to her side. "How are you, sweetheart? I wanted to come sooner, but I couldn't get away." A tray with an empty plate and a large glass of water sat on the small table beside her.

"Hi, Miss Tessa. I'm doing good. The doctor said my burn is healing well. I just have to be careful not to rub it or bump it on anything."

Tessa looked at Esther's leg. The large blister still extended from above the knee to the top of her foot. A light bandage covered it. Relief flowed through her. She'd been concerned about how the burn would look.

"It looks much better than it did at first." Cliff stood beside her.

"The angry red has faded. We're so grateful the blister didn't break. It could have so easily. God was with Wanda and Anthony. They had to get her into the carriage." He shook his head. "If they'd knocked it on something and tore it open, we'd have a completely different story, maybe a fever and serious illness. You know, Anthony had only learned to drive a week before to help with the threshing. He'd only driven the carriage on the road once."

Tessa shook her head. "That's amazing. God is so good." She patted Esther's arm. "I'm relieved you're getting better."

"I slept last night without that nasty medicine. It made me feel horrible. I don't want any more of that stuff." Esther made a face. "The doctor said I could quit taking it as long as I sleep well and don't roll around. At first, my leg hurt so much, I couldn't lie still."

Mrs. Dickenson walked into the sunroom. "It's already warm out here. I'm afraid it'll get too hot before we're home from church. Cliff, why don't you carry her into the sitting room, it'll be cooler. Here, I'll hold her leg." She turned to Tessa. "She has to keep her leg straight. If she bends it, it might tear the blister."

Tessa nodded. She stood back as Cliff lifted Esther, with Grandma Dickenson's help, then followed them into the house and down the hall to the sitting room.

Cliff lowered Esther into a chair beside an open window and propped her leg on a footstool. "We won't be gone long."

Tessa sat in a chair beside Esther and looked into her face. "We'll be fine won't we?" She turned toward Cliff. "You go and enjoy the service."

Cliff gazed at her and their eyes met. "I know you'll be alright. You understand Esther better than any of us."

Grandma brought a glass of water in and sat it on the lamp table as Grandpa descended the stairs. "Here, Esther, you need to drink this full glass while we're gone. The doctor said you should drink lots of water."

Esther wrinkled her nose. "Okay, if I have to."

"Yes, you have to." Her grandma swept from the room. Cliff smiled then followed her.

Tessa looked at Esther as Mr. and Mrs. Dickenson, Cliff, and Anthony left the house. "What would you like to do while they're gone?" She glanced around. "I loved playing games with my sisters. What games do you have?"

"Look in there." Esther pointed to the bookcase. There was a cabinet with drawers on the bottom. "We got a new game. It's called *Eckha*. Anthony played it with me."

Tessa pulled open the drawer. "We had this game at the Topeka Harvey House. I played it a couple of times." She took it out of the cupboard and looked around. "What do you play on? We need a flat surface."

"Over there." Esther pointed again.

A square wooden board leaned against the wall. Checker squares were painted on it. "Oh, that's perfect." Tessa retrieved it and placed it on Esther's lap, careful to avoid her injured leg.

"My grandpa made it. We play games on it a lot."

They soon had the game set up. Esther grabbed the yellow playing pieces. "I like red best, but my burn was too red. I want my leg to return to the right color."

Tessa chuckled at Esther's logic. "I guess you're right. What color should I choose?"

"You be green. I miss the grass. I'll be glad when I can get outside."

"Actually, the grass looks more like your playing pieces. We need rain to green it up. You play first."

They were soon engrossed in the strategy of moving their tokens across the board. Esther laughed heartily as she made a move and jumped three of Tessa's tokens.

"You little rascal. That was an impressive play." Tessa winked as she jumped two and landed her piece in the marked area on the opposite side of the board.

Esther frowned in concentration as she studied the board. Then she grinned as she jumped two. "I'm gonna win."

"We'll see."

They played on until Esther moved her last token into position on Tessa's side. "Yay! I won! I won!" She waved her arm in the air. "Let's play again."

"Yes, you did win, but don't get too carried away. Now, you need to drink that water. We don't want any left when your grandma gets home. We'll play another game when that water's all gone."

"I don't like water." Esther wrinkled her nose as she picked up the glass and drank one swallow.

"But you want to get well. The water will help your burn heal."

Esther drank half the glass while Tessa gathered the playing pieces and began setting them up again. "Set your side up, then finish the water. We're not going to play until every drop is gone."

"Aww." Esther set the glass on the lamp table and set up her pieces. Reluctantly, she drank the rest of the water. "Now I have to pee."

Tessa looked around. "How do we do that?"

Esther pointed toward a stool with a chamber pot lid. "Grandpa made a stool for me to sit on. If you will help me up I can stand on my good leg and turn around to sit on it."

Tessa lifted the lid to reveal the chamber pot below. "What a clever idea. Someone should have thought of this a long time ago. That's handy."

With Tessa's help, Esther was soon back in the chair.

Tessa heaved a sigh of relief. "Whew. I'm glad we got that done. Should I empty it in the outhouse?"

"No. Pa will get it later. Let's play another game."

Tessa moved her last piece in place as the family trooped back in. "I won!" She grinned at Esther. "We both won a game. Now we're even."

Esther nodded. "That was fun. Thank you for staying with me, Miss Tessa. I love it when you're here."

Just then Anna and Charlie ran into the room. Anna threw her arms around her sister. "I missed you, sissy."

Cliff followed them. "Be careful, Anna. Remember what I told you in the carriage. Don't touch Esther's leg."

Tessa picked Charlie up so he could see his sister. "Just look. Don't touch. You can tell your sissy hi."

Grandma Dickenson and Cora walked in as Tessa set Charlie down. She began to gather the playing pieces and put the game away.

"How did things go?" Mildred swept a look around the room. "I see you drank your water."

Tessa smiled. "We got along great. We played two games of *Eckha*. I won once and Esther won once."

"And she helped me to the commode." Esther grinned at Tessa.

"I forgot to tell you about that."

"It's okay. We did fine."

Cora stepped up. "You look perky today, Esther. I love to see that smile on your face." She picked up the wooden game board and placed it against the wall. "Let's fix dinner. I'm hungry."

Soon the tantalizing odor of fried chicken wafted through the house. Tessa helped by setting the table.

Cliff carried Esther in to sit at the table and propped her

leg on a low stool. He patted her shoulder. "I'm glad you're feeling better."

After a dinner of fried chicken, mashed potatoes and gravy, green beans, and a vegetable salad, they had fresh cherry pies. "Yum. This is delicious. Are these cherries from your tree?"

"They're actually from Cliff's farm. We picked and canned them last month." Mildred took a bite.

Tessa looked at Cliff. "Really? Do you have other fruit trees?"

"I have two apple trees and two cherry trees. The apples will be ready soon." He smiled. "Anthony and I need to head to the farm and do chores. Would you like to ride along? You could see where we live."

"I'd love to see your farm." Excitement rushed through Tessa. "Let me help clean up here first."

"You go on ahead. Cora can help me." Mrs. Dickenson rose and began clearing the table.

Cliff picked up Esther. "Come on. I'll take this gal into the sitting room then we'll leave. Those cows are probably wondering what's happened to us."

CHAPTER 9

On their way out of town, Cliff and Tessa sat on the front seat, with Anthony in the back. Cliff took a deep breath. "It's good to be back in the country." He chuckled. "I do appreciate all Mildred has done to help with Esther's care. But she's a bit domineering. She thinks she's in charge of everyone. I'll be glad when Esther's well enough to go back home."

"She'll need someone to help her get around for a while."

Cliff sighed. "I know."

Anthony leaned forward. "I can help her. I'll be happy to get back home, too."

"I know you will, son. You're a tremendous helper. I don't know how I would've managed without you."

Tessa looked around at the grass-covered rolling hillocks on each side of the dirt road. There were very few trees. "What caused all these little hills? I haven't seen anything like them."

"They're sand dunes that were formed years ago. They're covered by grass now, but if the grass is disturbed the sand will still blow in the wind. We often have prairie fires that come through. The fire will burn the grass. Then the dunes blow and shift."

"Fires? That sounds scary."

"They can be scary. I keep a fireguard plowed around my farm during the dry season. But I didn't bring you out here to scare you. Although the fires come periodically, we've never been seriously threatened. I have quite a bit of farm ground that doesn't have grass on it so that helps."

Tessa's shoulders relaxed as she gazed at the seemingly endless sky. "You can see forever out here, from horizon to horizon. I like the blue sky with white fleecy clouds. It's so different from the hills and trees of Arkansas."

"It's one of my favorite things about this country. You'll see trees around farmsteads and along creeks, but that's about all." Cliff took Tessa's hand in his. "I hope you like our farm."

"I'm sure I will. I grew up on a farm."

A few minutes later, Anthony pointed. "There it is. Look, Sassy is by the corral gate waiting for me. Can I walk her some after we get the cows milked?"

"That's a good idea. I want to show Miss Tessa the house."

Tessa gazed at the neat farmstead. The white single-story house welcomed her from a distance. Beside it was a garden plot. It had been plowed and a few plants struggled to survive. She'd love to enlarge it and bring it back to life with vegetables and flowers.

Farther back on the property was a large barn, two granaries, and another smaller shed. Cows grazed in a pasture behind the barn and several horses stood in a paddock beside the garden. Tessa smiled at the sight of a chicken house with chickens running around a fenced-in area. A warm glow filled her. It all reminded her of home, and she yearned to give it some motherly touches.

"What do you think?" Cliff squeezed her hand as he turned into the lane which led to the house.

"Oh, Cliff, I love it! Everything looks so homey. I don't know how you've kept it up so well and cared for the children."

"It doesn't look as tidy as it did when Ella was alive. She had flowers growing everywhere, and the garden was a masterpiece. I haven't been able to keep up with that, although I tried. I plowed and planted it, and we got a handful of vegetables from it, a pitiful showing."

Tessa laughed. "It does look like it needs some attention. That's one thing I miss about living on the farm. We had a large garden."

Cliff pulled up to the front of the house. "I need to go in and get the milk bucket. Would you rather stay here at the house, or do you want to come to the barn while we do the chores?"

"Oh, I want to go to the barn with you. I want to see the cows and chickens. It's good to be back on a farm." She chuckled. "Since my daddy only had girls, I learned to milk the cows when he couldn't."

Cliff grinned. "You are a farm girl, aren't you?" He clucked to Babe and drove on to the shed beside the barn. "Anthony, you bring the cows in and I'll give Babe her grain. You can feed the other horses when you walk Sassy."

Tessa watched as Cliff poured half a bucket of wheat in a trough for the mare. He worked with the confidence of familiarity. Soon they were on the way into the barn.

Anthony had one cow in the stall and was leading the other one through the door. "They were waiting and bawling at the door. I'm sure they're more than ready to be milked. Their udders are full."

Cliff grabbed the stool and sat down beside the first one. He patted her flank. "This is Bossy. She thinks she needs to be first." He started shooting the milk into the bucket in two rhythmic streams. "The other one is Bessie."

Anthony scattered hay in their food troughs.

Tessa leaned down and picked up one of the kittens that crowded around his feet and snuggled it in her arms. "I love kittens. They're so soft and cuddly. They're fun to watch, too, when they're playing." She laughed and set the cat back down as Cliff began squirting milk at the mama and her babies. They drank the milk mid-stream, their little faces white with the overflow.

He aimed the milk back into the bucket. "I'll give them some in their pan before we go to the house." Before long, the bucket was half-full, and he moved to Bessie.

Tessa walked to the door and looked out onto the pasture while she waited. Cliff had quite a herd of cows and half-grown calves. She wanted to be a part of all this.

Ten minutes later, they had turned the milk cows out to graze and were headed toward the house. Tessa looked around. "I'd like to see the chickens. Are there eggs? I'll collect them."

Cliff waved toward the house. "Let me take this milk inside and get the egg basket. I'll meet you there. Gertrude, our pet chicken, will be delighted to make your acquaintance."

Tessa smiled. "Pet chicken? I've never heard of a pet chicken."

Anthony took her hand. "Come and see. She'll come right up to you."

Sure enough, as they walked toward the fence, a sleek brown chicken ran to greet them. Anthony opened the gate and slipped inside then motioned for Tessa to follow. "Here, pick her up. She loves to be held."

Tessa pulled the gate shut behind her then reached down and picked up the hen. Gertrude settled into her arms, quite content. "I can't believe this. How did you tame her?"

"She's been like that since she was a baby chick. She would run to us, jump up on our knees, then climb up our arms to sit on our shoulders. She'll still sit on your shoulder, but she's getting kind of big. Esther loves her and carries her all over the farm."

"I love it." Tessa stroked Gertrude's feathers. She had not only fallen in love with Cliff and his children, but she also loved his farm. *God, I hope I'm reading your will correctly. I want to be a part of this little family.*

"What do you think of her?" Cliff walked toward the chicken pen.

"It's amazing! I've never seen anything like it. Our chickens scattered when we entered their yard."

"I guess Anthony told you. She has been that way since she hatched from the egg."

Tessa handed Gertrude to Anthony and reached for the egg basket. "Here, I'll collect the eggs." She made her way into the chicken coop and searched through the nesting boxes attached to the wall. She found the eggs nestled among the straw and placed them gently in the basket. This had been her and her sister's job since she could remember. She smiled as she moved back into the sunshine. "I found eight eggs." Tessa lifted her skirt as she stepped carefully across the chicken yard.

"That's about what we've been getting every day. Some of the hens aren't laying. Maybe because of the heat." Cliff poured grain into the chicken's feed trough.

Anthony carried a bucket of water from the pump and dumped it in a water pan. "Can I go walk Sassy now? We've finished the chores."

"Sure. Miss Tessa and I will go to the house." He turned to Tessa. "That is if you want to. I need to strain the milk, and I'd like to show you inside. I haven't had a chance to clean since Esther was hurt so it's sort of messy."

"Yes. I want to see your house."

They walked to the back door which led to a screened-in

porch. Cliff opened it and took her elbow to escort her. Tessa looked around. There were laundry tubs stacked in one corner and a table with a water bucket sat beside it. A dipper hung from a nail on the wall. On the other side was an icebox.

They passed through to the kitchen. Cliff took the egg basket and set it on the table. Sunlight shone in the windows which gave the room a cheery glow. Tessa noticed that there were dirty soup bowls in the dry sink and the soup pot still sat on the cold cook stove.

Cliff waved his arm around. "As you can see, the children left the dirty dishes in their haste to get Esther into town. And I haven't taken the time to wash them when I came out to do chores."

Tessa glanced around. "Is there an apron? Let's get them washed. It won't take long. You don't want them sitting here the whole time you're in town with Esther." She picked up a pitcher that sat nearby. "Here, go get some water and we'll let it heat while you show me around." She peeked into the soup pot. "There's still soup in here. You don't want to save it do you? It's been sitting here for several days. Why don't you give it to the chickens? They'll appreciate it."

Cliff laughed outright. He took her shoulders and turned her to face him. "You're a regular little housewife, aren't you?"

Tessa sobered and looked up at him. "I'm sorry. I didn't mean to be bossy. I had no right."

"No, no. I love it. This house has needed a woman's touch for far too long." He looked into her eyes. "Tessa, would you consider marrying me? I've loved you since the moment I laid eyes on you. The way you looked at Esther melted my heart. Do you think you could ever love an old farmer like me?"

"You aren't old Cliff, and I do love you!" Joy bubbled up inside her into a happy smile. "I first fell in love with your precious children. Esther stole my heart immediately, then

Anna, Charlie, and Anthony." She frowned slightly. "I wasn't sure about my feelings for you. It happened so quickly, and I didn't see how we could have a relationship with my work commitment. But now I know. I belong here with you and your family."

"Are you sure? You'll have to give up a lot--the prestige and the opportunity to travel. Being a Harvey Girl is special."

"It is, and I don't take it lightly, but I'm convinced God wants me here for you." She hesitated. "I mostly wanted to support my family with my job."

"We can still help your family--I have money in the bank." He took her hands. "Most importantly, I refuse to have a marriage of convenience. I don't want to marry someone to take care of my children and my house. It has to be a real marriage...a life of mutual love."

Tessa gazed at his earnest face. Love and admiration swept through her. "I do love you, Cliff. God has filled my heart to overflowing with love for you. I want to be your real and true wife as long as He allows."

Cliff put his arms around her and pulled her close. Tessa lifted her lips for his kiss. Joy and ecstasy made her knees weak. She didn't know a kiss could be so overwhelming. As she leaned against him for support, she became aware of his firm muscles and steadily beating heart. She was lost in the rapture of the moment.

He pulled back and looked into her eyes. Tessa could see his love shining there. He pulled her close again. "I've waited for this for so long. I love you, Tessa, more than I can tell you."

Tessa rested against his chest and marveled at the incredible goodness of God who had brought them together.

Finally, Cliff released her and stepped back. He chuckled. "I guess we better get some things done around here. That wasn't how I envisioned I'd ask you to marry me. It just happened."

Tessa smiled. "It was perfect."

He took her hand. "Let me show you the rest of the house, then we can get this kitchen cleaned up."

Tessa looked around as they walked into the parlor. It was pleasingly arranged. A large stone fireplace dominated the end of the room with a floral-patterned wood-framed sofa, two chairs, and a lamp table situated around the room. Green drapes hung at the windows. A bookcase filled with books and games sat against one of the walls. Tessa sighed. "This is so welcoming. I'm sure you do a lot of living in this room."

"We spend a lot of time here." Cliff pointed toward a door beside the fireplace. "That's my room." There were two more doors in the far wall. "Anthony has his room, and Esther, Anna, and Charlie sleep together there." He indicated the room toward the front of the house. "They have a hard time keeping their things put away. I'm sure their room needs to be cleaned."

Tessa nodded. "That's typical. My little sisters and brother have trouble with that, too." They walked back into the kitchen.

They worked together and soon had the dirty dishes and soup pot washed and put away. They strained the milk into a crock. "We'll take the milk and eggs back into town. They'll spoil before we get back, and Mildred can use them to help feed our brood."

Before long, they were on their way into town. Tessa's heart skipped a beat when Cliff reached to take her hand. She wasn't sure how everything would work out, but she knew God had it in His hands.

CLIFF STOOD in a wide stance with his hands behind his back and watched anxiously as Doctor Snyder removed the bandage from Esther's leg. The blister had gone down and appeared to be dry brown skin. The redness around it had nearly disappeared. He breathed a sigh of relief. He hadn't seen it for several days and wasn't sure what to expect.

The doctor stood and placed his instruments in his bag. "Well, young lady, I think you're well on your way back to normal. Your leg still needs to heal, but we're past the critical period." He tousled her hair. "Maybe it would be better to let someone older carry the hot soup. At least, until you've grown a little more."

Esther nodded. "Yes, sir, I will."

Cliff stepped forward. "So, do you think it'd be alright to take her back to the farm?"

Mrs. Dickenson had been standing beside Esther's chair. "Don't you think it would be wise to keep her here another week, John? We wouldn't want her to have a backset."

The doctor winked as he turned to face Cliff. "That won't be necessary. She can go home. That's the best place for her. I think it would be wise to keep a loose bandage on the burned area for another week or so just to protect it, but she should be able to walk short distances."

Anthony stepped forward. "I'll help her. I'm ready to get back to the farm."

Doctor Snyder smiled. "I bet you are. This has been a long stretch. Thanks to you and your quick thinking, your sister didn't get the fever. That's a huge blessing."

"I'm thankful, too!" Cliff grinned and put his arm around his son's shoulders.

Anthony stretched to his full height, a pleased expression on his face.

The doctor picked up his bag. "Well, guess I'll be on my

way. Oh, and bring Esther to my office for a follow-up check in a week. We need to make sure things are proceeding as they should." He hummed the first few bars of "Amazing Grace" as he strode from the room. A few seconds later they heard him leave through the sunroom door.

"Well, wouldn't that just start you up the road!?" Mildred huffed as she hustled around the chair. "He left without a 'by-your-leave.' Are you sure you're ready to take all these children to that farm? I could keep the little ones until you get settled in."

Cliff worked to keep a straight face. "We'll be fine. I appreciate all you've done. You've been a life-saver, but now we need to get things back to normal. I'm sure all the kids are ready to go." He began to gather Esther's clothes as Anthony ran from the room and up the stairs.

"Here, let me get those if you have to leave." Mrs. Dickenson took the items from his hand. "You get your things together."

An hour later, Cliff felt light with anticipation as he steered the carriage toward the Harvey House. He'd stopped by the General Store to pick up a few supplies. Now he was on his way to get Anna and Charlie and to see Tessa.

The last three weeks had been exhausting. It would be a huge relief to get his family back together on the farm. If only Tessa could go with them it would be perfect. He grinned. In a few weeks, she'd be there to stay. That was the one good thing that had resulted from Esther's accident. Tessa had realized she loved him and wanted to marry him.

Cliff guided Babe into the Santa Fe Hotel parking lot and reined her in at the hitching rail.

Esther scooted forward on her seat. "I want to go in and see Miss Tessa and Aunt Cora."

"Oh, no, you don't." Cliff reached back and pushed her

back onto the seat. "You don't need to be walking on that foot just yet. You stay out here with Anthony. I'll go get Anna and Charlie. Maybe Miss Tessa and Aunt Cora can come out here to see you."

Anthony turned around to face his sister. "I told Doctor Snyder I'd take care of you. We'll wait out here."

Esther frowned and crossed her arms. "I'm okay. The doctor said so, and besides, you aren't my boss."

Cliff put his finger under her chin. "But I am. And I said for you to stay put."

He shook his head, a slight smile on his face as he walked up the steps to the wrap-around porch. God had given him exceptional children, but sometimes he needed the wisdom of Solomon to know how to deal with them. There hadn't been time to talk about his marriage to Tessa with all that had been going on. Hopefully, Anthony would be alright with it.

Charlie burst out the Harvey House door and wrapped his arms around his daddy's legs. The screen door clattered shut behind him. "Daddy, Daddy, come see the picture I drawed."

Cliff picked him up. "By all means, let's go see it." He opened the door and entered the cool lobby. "Are you ready to go home?"

Charlie pushed back. "And Anna, and Esther, and Anthony?"

"We're all going."

"Yippee!" Charlie scrambled out of Cliff's arms and ran across the lobby to Cora's office. "Anna, we're goin' home."

Cora walked toward Cliff. "So, the doctor gave his approval?"

Cliff nodded. "The burn looks so much better. The blister has gone down and most of the redness is gone. We just have to keep it covered for the next week to protect it." He chuckled. "I couldn't believe it. Your mom wanted to keep her for another week."

"She likes to feel needed."

"Well, she was a blessing for sure, but it's time to get back to normal." He glanced toward the dining room. "Is Tessa available? I told Esther I'd have you two come out and say hi."

"She should be free. We're done with the morning rush, and I'm sure she's set up for lunch. Go get her, and I'll get Anna and Charlie. I thought you might be going so I packed their belongings this morning."

Tessa appeared at the dining-room door as Cliff headed in that direction. His heart thumped wildly as their vision collided. The welcome in her smiling eyes nearly knocked him off his feet. Without thinking he took her hands. "Tessa, we're going home. The doctor said Esther's healed enough to go to the farm. We still have to be careful, but she is over the critical time."

"That's wonderful news. I know everyone's more than ready to go. Anna and Charlie have been talking about Gertrude and the kitty cats."

"I wish you were going, but it won't be long. Just over two weeks till the wedding. Pray for me. I haven't had a chance to talk to the kids about it."

"Cliff, you need to do that!"

"I know. I'll tell them today."

"There's Daddy."

Cliff and Tessa turned as Charlie and Anna ran toward them.

Cora followed them with a bag and a box in her hands. She handed them to Cliff. "Here are the children's clothes and toys. I put the pictures they drew in there. They wanted you to see them. And Sam, our head cook, fixed a meal for you to take home. I'm not sure what all he put in, but I know there are sandwiches and cookies. He said you wouldn't have time to fix dinner when you got home."

Cliff stood still, stunned. "Really? That's incredible. I'll pay you for it."

"No. He wanted to do it. It's on Fred Harvey's tab. He told Mr. McKinsey to help you in any way we could."

"I'll never be able to repay him and everyone here for all you've done to help me during this time. Please tell Sam, and Mr. McKinsey and Mr. Harvey thank you for me."

"I will. Now let's go out and see Esther so you can be on your way."

Cliff carried Charlie and Anna put her arms up to Tessa to be held as they trooped out to the carriage.

A short while later they were on their way. As they left the city, Cliff took a deep breath and let it out slowly. It was good to get out into the wide-open spaces. Suddenly he stilled as he heard Esther's loud whisper behind him.

"Anna, wanna know a secret? I think Miss Tessa's gonna be our new ma, at least I hope so. Pa likes her a lot. Did you see how he stared at her?"

"You sure?"

"Pretty sure."

Anthony swiveled toward him. "Is that true, Pa? Are you going to marry Miss Tessa?"

Cliff cringed at the accusing tone in Anthony's voice. He swallowed as he searched for words. "Yes, son, I asked her to marry me and she said yes. I need a wife. It's nothing against your ma, but she isn't here. She's in Heaven. I need somebody I can love here, now. I'm sorry I didn't tell you sooner. There just wasn't an opportunity."

Cliff sent a quick prayer heavenward as Anthony turned and stared at the road in front of them. *Dear, Lord, please give me the right words. I need your wisdom right now.* He searched for words as the silence stretched on.

Finally, Anthony shifted toward him on the seat. "Does she love you?"

"Yes, she does. It's a miracle, but God has filled her heart with love."

"Does she love me, and Esther, and Anna, and Charlie?"

"She loves you all very much. And she loves our farm."

"Does she love God?"

"She loves God and wants to serve Him."

Anthony crossed his arms and shrugged his shoulders. "Then I guess she has to be our new ma. That's what you said she needed to do."

Cliff nodded. "I did, didn't I? God answered my prayers."

Anthony sighed. "If we can't have our real ma, I guess Miss Tessa will do."

"Yippee!" Esther bounced on the seat. "See I told you, Anna."

Cliff grinned at the happy cheers behind him. He put his arm around Anthony's shoulders and hugged him. God was good!

CHAPTER 10

It was still dark outside when Tessa awoke. The days were getting shorter. It was Saturday, September fifth, her wedding day. She stared out the window at the brightly shining moon. Her thoughts tumbled about in her head.

When she and Cliff had declared their intention to get married, Mr. McKinsey had written to Fred Harvey and explained the family situation. Much to Tessa's surprise, Fred Harvey had answered and given her his blessing. He was even planning to attend the marriage celebration this afternoon. He'd offered to give her away but instead had issued passes for her family to come when she expressed the desire to have her father do the honor. Tessa shook her head. She could hardly believe that Pa and her sisters were here in the Santa Fe Hotel, in a room on the floor below her. It was more than she could have imagined.

Esther's leg was almost completely healed and Cliff had moved back to the farm. Tessa and Cora had taken a day off and cleaned the house when they found out Cliff's parents were coming from Ohio. The wedding gave them a good excuse to come see their grandchildren.

Tessa rolled over and threw back the sheet. There was a bit of a chill in the air. She pushed her legs out and sat on the side of the bed. Hannah would be up soon since she had to work this morning.

Tessa felt a small pang of regret. Yesterday, she worked her last day. She'd enjoyed the camaraderie of working with the other girls and the prestige of serving in the Harvey House. It would be bittersweet to turn in her uniforms, but when she thought of Cliff and his children, she knew it was the right decision. She was happiest when she was on the farm with them.

She pushed her feet into her slippers and shuffled down the hall to the bathroom. She grinned, realizing she might miss the water closet and the warm water in the reservoir for baths. Maybe Cliff could figure out a way to bring water into the house.

When she returned to the room, Hannah was sitting on the side of her bed. "You got up before me this morning. You must be excited! I would be." She shook her head. "Just think, Fred Harvey is going to be here. That's amazing."

"I know. And I've only been a Harvey Girl for three months. He cares about all of us." Tessa chuckled. "It does make me a little nervous, though."

"I wouldn't worry. Cora didn't think he was upset about you getting married to Cliff." Hannah shrugged. "It just seems like the right thing to do. God put you two together and gave you a love for his children."

She turned toward the wardrobe where Tessa's dress hung. "I'm glad you had a new dress made. It's so pretty on you. The dark green is much better than black."

"I think so, too." Tessa picked up her hairbrush and began to brush her hair. "I wish Elise could have come. She had to work this weekend. I wanted you to meet her. My oldest sister, Margaret, will stand up with me."

Hannah stood and pulled her robe around her. "I better get ready for work. I'll see you and your family at breakfast. When is Cliff coming in?"

"He'll probably come before dinner. His brother, Paul, plans to be here from southern Kansas this morning. He's going to stand up with Cliff."

AFTER DINNER, Tessa and her sisters, Margaret, Abigail, and Theresa, walked up the stairs to her room. Tessa's little sister, Lucile, was with Esther in Cora's office. The two had quickly become friends.

Tessa sighed. "I'm glad you and Pa came to my wedding. I wish Ma, Betsy, and Samuel could have come. I hoped I'd get to see them."

Margaret nodded. "Ma wanted to come, but she couldn't travel that far with her bad back. It would've been too difficult to keep track of Betsy and Samuel. Ma wasn't surprised that you were getting married, though. She figured you'd find a man."

"I didn't intend to. I planned to work out my contract, but Cliff and his children captured my heart. Anna and Charlie reminded me of Betsy and Samuel, Esther stole my heart, and then before I knew it I'd fallen in love with Cliff."

Theresa giggled. "I saw Cliff's son Anthony. He's cute! I wouldn't mind getting better acquainted with him."

"You're just a hopeless romantic." Abigail brushed her sister with her arm.

"No, I'm not." Theresa pushed her back. "I'll get married to a good-looking man, and you'll still be waiting."

"Now, girls." Margaret got between them. "We aren't here to argue. We're here to help Tessa get ready for her wedding. Come on, settle down."

They walked into Tessa's room.

"This is nice." Abigail looked around. "I think I may become a Harvey Girl when I get old enough. I'll be sixteen next March."

"It would be a good job for you. Fred Harvey is great to work for and the benefits are fantastic."

Margaret walked to the wardrobe. "Is this the dress you're going to wear? It's pretty. I brought my burgundy one. They'll look nice together." She closed Tessa's half-filled trunk. "Here sit on this, and I'll fix your hair then I'll get my dress on."

Tessa smiled as she sat down. "It's nice having you here to help me. I've missed you all, so much." She waved toward her dress. "I splurged and had Betty, at the dress and millinery shop, make it for me. She also fashioned the hat that matches. She wanted me to get a new bustle and petticoats, but I didn't have that much money. I'll just have to use my old ones." She laughed. "It's the first dress I ever had that Ma or I didn't sew."

Margaret brushed Tessa's hair up into a loose chignon with a bun on the top of her head. "Your green hat will look elegant with your blonde hair. I'm happy for you, Sis. Cliff seems like an outstanding man."

"He is so thoughtful and kind, and he's such a good father to his children. I feel very fortunate."

Just then, there was a knock at the door and Elise Dumond stuck her head around the door frame. "Hello. Is this the right room? I heard a lot of chattering in here."

Tessa jumped up and rushed across the room. "Elise! You did make it! I was so sad when you said you had to work and couldn't come." Tessa threw her arms around her friend in a hug, then turned to her sisters. "This is my best friend, Elise

Dumond. We met at our Harvey Girl interview and then were roommates during training." She faced Elise. "It's so good to see you."

"It's good to see you, too. Mr. Ramsey and Della, our head waitress, told me yesterday that I could come. I came on the morning train." Elise smiled at Tessa. "Cora introduced me to Cliff. He's very handsome."

"He is, isn't he? He's also the most thoughtful and kind man I've ever known. And he has four amazing children."

"How did this all come about?" Elise glanced at Tessa's sisters. "Tell me your story while you get dressed. You need to get ready."

Abigail picked up the bustle and tied the attached strings to Tessa's waist.

"I saw Cliff and his family the first night I arrived in Hutchinson. They sat beside me at the lunch counter and ate supper. I was drawn to his daughter, Esther. She wouldn't eat her meal and appeared to be sad. Later, I learned that Cliff's wife, Cora's sister, had died at the time of his youngest child, Charlie's, birth. I sympathized with Esther. I had to take a lot of responsibility for my sister's and our home when Mom injured her back and had to convalesce. I began to spend time with Esther whenever possible."

Tessa paused as Margaret tied her petticoat and slipped the dress over her head. "I didn't think a relationship between Cliff and me could develop since I'd signed the Harvey Girl contract, plus he was older with four children. Sooner than I could imagine, my feelings began to change. When Edward came by on his way to New Mexico, I realized I'd never care for him as I did for Cliff.

"Then Esther was burned. During that ordeal, God revealed where my heart belonged. When Cliff asked me to marry him, God gave me perfect peace about leaving my job to become his wife. I knew I loved him, and that he loved and needed me. Mr. McKinsey contacted Fred Harvey, and we got his blessing."

"I saw that Fred Harvey was here."

"Yes, we talked this morning. He was very understanding. He wanted to make sure this was what I wanted."

Abigail smoothed the dress and Margaret placed the hat on Tessa's head and secured it with hat pins.

Tessa stared in the mirror over her dresser. The dress fit her to perfection. The green taffeta flowed smoothly in front and fit her small waist. It had small ruffles at the neck and the ends of the sleeves. In the back, the fabric was gathered over the bustle, sending a cascade of graceful folds to the floor. The hat was the latest style, accented by a matching green taffeta bow. Tessa sucked in her breath. "It's perfect! The prettiest dress I've ever owned."

Margaret smiled and nodded as Abigail and Theresa gathered around. "It's breathtaking. Cliff will be swept off his feet." She looked at the clock on Tessa's dresser. "One-fifteen. We have forty-five minutes. You visit with Elise, and I'll get dressed then come get you. Why don't you other girls go down and see if there's anything you can do to help?"

Tessa motioned to Elise. "Let's wait in the upstairs parlor. We can sit in there." They laughed as they smoothed the voluminous amount of material to sit without wrinkling their skirts.

Tessa gazed at her friend. "It's so good to see you. Tell me about Emporia. Have you heard from Daniel?"

Elise frowned. "Not a word. I wish I'd hear. I hope he's safe." She relaxed her shoulders. "Daniel's family came into the Harvey House the other day. They hadn't heard from him either." She smiled. "His little niece, Elizabeth, is quite a character. His mother's in poor health and had some sort of an attack while they were there. I doubt it's easy for her to care for Elizabeth."

Her face fell. "My youngest brother, Jule, fell from a horse and broke his leg. He was unconscious for a while. I haven't heard anymore so I don't know how he is."

Shortly after one-thirty, Margaret reappeared. She was elegant in her burgundy dress. "Are you nervous? There's a lot of people gathered in the lobby."

Tessa shrugged. "It's a bit scary. I just pray that everything goes well."

"I saw Cora before I came up. She said everything's ready. Mr. Harvey is talking to Cliff and the minister."

They descended the broad staircase. As they paused on the second-floor landing, Tessa scanned the crowd. Besides their families, there were many church members as well as Harvey House staff and railroad workers. She blinked back tears. Cliff was well-loved in this community and she'd already made many friends in the Fred Harvey family.

Elise gave her a light hug. "I'll go down and find a seat. Relax and enjoy. This is your special day."

Tessa smiled as the community band began playing the Wedding March. She could distinctly hear the Civil War drummer keeping time with the music. Hutchinson was a wonderful city to make her home.

Margaret started down the stairs.

CLIFF STOOD at the end of the lobby, opposite the staircase, and gazed around the room at his family, friends, and neighbors. A thrill flowed through him. Tessa would walk down those stairs soon. He turned to his brother, Paul. "I'm glad you made it to stand up with me." He held out a ring. "Can you hold this? It was our grandmother's ring. Mother brought it. I wanted a different one from the one I gave Ella. "

"Sure, I'll keep it for you."

Cliff cuffed him on the shoulder. "It's been too long since we've been together."

Paul wrinkled his forehead. "I know. Although it's not that far away...the Rockin' M demands sunrise-to-sundown work. I've managed to establish and build up my herd, but it's a full-time job keeping the fences intact. The threat of poachers and free-loaders fill anything that resembles free-time." He smiled. "I've recently hired a couple of reliable ranch hands. That should give me more opportunity to get away. I'll bring my wife and children up sometime soon."

"We'd enjoy that."

"Cliff, I'd like you to meet Mr. Fred Harvey."

Cliff turned to see Cora headed toward him with a tall, well-dressed man at her side. "Hello, sir. I'm pleased to meet you." He smiled. "Sorry, I'm stealing one of your girls."

Mr. Harvey reached out to take Cliff's hand. "I hate losing good help, but she's assured me that she's in love and wants to marry you. You have my blessing."

"Thank you, sir. I appreciate that."

The minister walked up as Harvey found a seat. "It's time to get in place."

Tessa's friend, Elise, walked down the staircase and sat beside Cora. The community band began to play the Bridal March. Cliff scanned the crowd until he spied his four children beside their grandparents. Then Margaret, Tessa's sister, swept down the steps.

Cliff's heart pounded as he watched the top of the stairs. Tessa appeared, resplendent in her elegant green dress. Her blonde hair gleamed in the afternoon light. He couldn't keep the smile from his face as she descended. She looked his way and their eyes met. She was more beautiful than the evening he'd first caught sight of her.

At the bottom of the stairs, she met her father, and they walked toward him. Happiness flooded through Cliff as he took her hand, and they repeated their vows. He placed the ring on her finger then, upon being pronounced man and wife, took her in his arms and kissed her.

He felt a warm little body press against him and another. He released Tessa and looked down to see Anna and Charlie attached to his legs. Esther hugged Tessa, and Anthony walked toward them.

Tessa turned and gathered them all in a huge embrace. "I'm the happiest woman in the whole world, with the best family ever."

Cliff looked toward Heaven. *Thank you, Lord! You've answered my prayers beyond my expectations. You turned inconvenient love into true love so we could have a real marriage and a loving home.*

There was no question of the adoration in Tessa's eyes as he drew his whole family into his arms.

ACKNOWLEDGMENTS

Ginny Polentz and Tina Lusby — I treasure your friendships and I appreciate your taking the time to critique and edit the manuscript for Inconvenient Love. I know it probably seems like an eternity since I asked for your help with this. This last year has been crazy with all the distractions, but here we are with the finished product. Thank you so much for your love and support.

Peggy Lee Manoogian, Barbara Bettis, Connie Baker, and Janna Wiseley — Thank you for reading, editing, and making helpful corrections and suggestions. You have had an important part in this process.

Fellow members of my writing groups: Mozarks ACFW (American Christian Fiction Writers), Ozark Romance Writers, and Women's Get-Away Writer's Retreat — Even though we have had to meet much of this last year remotely, by Zoom and live stream, I have been encouraged by your support, instruction, and inspiration. It is a blessing to be able to meet back together in person. I finished the manuscript for this novella while at the *Women's Get-Away Writer's Retreat* in March 2020, right before the shutdown. I'm looking forward to seeing everyone again in November 2021.

Erik Smith — Thank you for taking the photographs for the cover. Once again you did an amazing job. *Janna Wiseley and Holly Smith* —Thank you for your support and for helping gather the props for the cover photo. *Kelly Smith* —Thank you for all you do to help and encourage me in this writing process. You created the cover, formatted and edited the manuscript, and published the book through Tallgrass Media. I can't thank you all enough. I couldn't do this without you!

Most of the information about the Harvey Girls and the Harvey Houses came from *The Harvey Girls; Women who opened the West* by Lesley Poling-Kempes, *The Harvey House Cookbook; Memories of Dining Along the Santa Fe Railroad* by George H. Foster and Peter C. Weiglin, and *Harvey Houses of Kansas; Historic Hospitality from Topeka to Syracuse* by Rosa Walston Latimer.

The Lord is my strength and song and is become my salvation.
Psalm 118:14

ABOUT THE AUTHOR

Joyce Valdois Smith is wife to Bob, mother to four married children and grandmother to twelve beautiful grandchildren. She is a retired public health and school nurse. Writing has been her long time passion. Joyce is an author of Christian historical and contemporary fiction as well as children's books. She lives with her husband and Cavalier King Charles Spaniel, Lady Catherine (Katie), in southwest Missouri.

Visit her online at: joycevaldoissmith.com